Hi Nigel,
I hope this
brings you J

Miracle Village

NADJEDA ESTRIPLET

A story by Nadjeda Estriplet

Edited by Jillian Ryan

Cover designed by Gabriel Akinrinmade

CONTENTS

Prologue   pg. 9

Chapter One   pg. 19

Chapter Two   pg. 39

Chapter Three   pg. 53

Chapter Four   pg. 67

Chapter Five   pg. 81

Chapter Six   pg. 105

Chapter Seven   pg. 117

Chapter Eight   pg. 127

Chapter Nine   pg. 137

Chapter Ten   pg. 153

Thank you, Ms. Whitley, for believing in me before I even knew what that meant. Thank you, Asha Appel, for showing me the power of writing. And thank you to all of my life teachers who have taught me more than I could have ever learned in a classroom.

Prologue

Mama, we're home!"

Jason pounded on the door, almost springing it from its hinges. He wiped the sweat from his forehead and let out an exasperated sigh. This Caribbean heat was killing him. He almost forgot how hot it could get out here. He could hardly catch his breath through the thick humidity. It had only been a few months since he had been on the island, yet his tolerance for the heat had lowered eminently.

Jason was here for a long overdue visit to his mother, his queen, his world, his heart. The trip was a surprise, until his big-mouthed big brother, Wesley, spilled the beans the week prior to their arrival.

Mama's excitement could be heard through the phone when the news broke that both her boys were coming home early for the summer.

Several hours had passed since Jason and Wesley landed in Port-au-Prince, Haiti, but it had taken them another two hours to find a ride to little Miracle Village, or as the natives called it *Vilaj Mirak*. The confusing hustle and bustle of the city in addition to their limited knowledge of the Creole language only made matters worse. Communicating with the airport staff and taxi drivers proved to be quite the task but somehow they were able to use the little bit of Creole that they knew to get by. When they finally found a "tap tap," willing to make the one and half hour trek, they lugged their suitcases onto the wagon, hopped into the already packed vehicle and hung on for dear life as it ricocheted over the rocky road. After what felt like a full day, the boys were relieved to make it to the little secluded community.

Miracle Village was a peculiar little town. It looked as though it did not belong to Haiti. It did not quite fit in and seemed to have no place there. The ground was mostly made up of gravel and the homes were small, simple, and uniformed. Each house was evenly spaced out and painted in a striking colorful hue. Mama's home in particular was red. Seated on the roof of each of these homes were large panels that glared in the sunlight; solar panels that powered energy throughout the town.

Miracle Village had the look and feel of a typical American suburb, the only difference being the level of affluence. In fact, some have joked that the town was airlifted from The States and placed on Haitian soil. Though it did not feel like home, the inhabitants of the town were thankful nonetheless. It was in a sense, a refuge.

Jason continued to knock on the door waiting for Mama to open up. It was strange that the door was even locked in the first place. She usually left the door open, so much so, that the boys never even bothered to get a key.

Jason's impatience was growing. He wanted nothing more than to see Mama and her bright smile. He could not wait to just hug her and love on her.

"Mama never locks the door, and she would never take this long to open up," said Wesley, his patience also wearing thin. He too could not wait to see his mother. He always teased his baby brother saying that he was the favorite and he had every intention of trying to prove it on this trip.

"Maybe she's sleeping," Wesley continued. He was standing next to Jason with his luggage trailing behind him.

"No, you already told Mama that we're coming so knowing her, she's probably up cleaning and cooking up a huge dinner for us."

Jason knocked again, now worried that something was wrong. The fears that lingered in the back of his mind began to creep over his thoughts. He often worried about his mother's wellbeing, almost to the point of obsession. If it were up to him, he would come visit his mother more regularly, but his hectic schedule left him with few liberties. Instead, he spent his time away from his mother concerned for her health and praying each day that he could be there for her if anything were to happen.

"Mama it's us!" Wesley screamed once more.

Just as Jason was about to go around the house and peep through one of the windows, the door suddenly flew open. However, instead of his mother's bright smile, Jason was face to face with an expressionless glower. He stared into eyes that did not belong to his family. A strange woman who he presumed was a native of the island looked at him with intent. Her eyes dark and as big as saucers, her skin smooth, silky, and glistening like honey, her body petite yet full, and her lips in a natural pout with a defined cupid's bow. Her hair, featherweight, dark and wavy, reaching just a little past her shoulders. She was ethereal. A soft gasp escaped Jason as he watched her blink. Her long lashes fanned down and then back up. Her eyes shone with a deep knowledge and he wondered a bit about her.

"Eske I konnen you?" Jason tried his best to use his broken Haitian Creole to ask the woman if he knew her. He was confused by her presence and temporarily maimed by her beauty

"No, you don't."

Jason was relieved to hear that the woman spoke English. Her voice was staid, authoritative, and for some reason, it lured him.

"Who are you?" Wesley chimed in, peeking around Jason who was blocking his view. He sounded a bit annoyed at whatever was happening between Jason and this woman. He just wanted to get out of this heat and get inside to see his Mama.

"I'm the nurse."

"Nurse?" Wesley, asked, a bit confused. He did not wait for clarification. "Where's my Mama?"

"My boys!"

His question was quickly answered as Mama came by the door to greet her sons.

"Mama!" they both exclaimed as they came in for a hug. She showered them with kisses one by one. Each time she finished with one, the other would come back for more. She could not help but to laugh at her silly boys. Although they were in their early 20's, they were still big kids at heart, and not a thing had changed, except for their height. They have always been tall like their father, but it seemed as though they grew even more since the last time she had seen them; about a year ago.

They towered over her stature and she could barely reach up to stroke their handsome faces. Both their slim fit frames encased her now rounder frame in a double hug and their long hair tickled her face. She hated it and had always begged them to cut their hair shorter, but they would never. It was part of "their look" they said. Either way, she tugged on their tresses affectionately teasing them.

The boys both stood back to take a good look at their Mama. Her fair skin seemed to glow under the sun and her hair was parted down the middle and plated into two long braids, her signature style. A few things had changed since the last time the boys had seen her. A few more wrinkles by her warm eyes, a couple of new lines framing her kind smile, some greys peeking through her hair, and definitely more belly for them to wrap their arms around. However, one thing that had not changed at all and would never change was her beauty.

"How was your flight my babies?" Mama spoke with a heavy accent coating her words.

"Long, but I'll do anything to come see you," said Jason.

"I would swim the sea to be here," Wesley replied, trying to one-up Jason's compliment.

"Oh my honeys, you boys are so silly! I am so happy that you are here! I have so much prepared for you!"

"Mama, you have a nurse?" asked Jason.

"Huh?" she replied, a bit confused.

"Yeah, she said she's your nurse," said Wesley, pointing to the woman who opened the door for them. She stood erect and seemingly on guard by the door. She came close to being forgotten amidst the joyous reunion, but her presence could not be dismissed.

Jason watched as his mother took in a deep breath. She seemed a bit nervous and he wondered why.

"Yeah baby, that's …umm, that's uh…that's ..."

"Detra…my name is Detra."

Chapter One

All three of them, Mama, Jason, and Wesley stood silent and stared at Detra for a short while before Wesley broke the barrier.

"Mama, you don't need a nurse," he said, "you're fine!"

"Well, baby, I haven't been feeling like myself lately. And De… ummm … Detra here, well…she's here to help make me feel better," Mama offered a tight smile.

Detra stood erect by the door as the three looked over at her. It looked as if they wanted some kind of explanation. She cleared her throat.

"I know your mother from church. And she needed a little help around here, so I'm here to help."

They all looked at her wide eyed for a moment before Wesley spoke up again.

"So you're Mama's nurse? From church? And you're also helping out around the house?" It sounded a bit fishy to him.

"Yes," replied Detra, with a soft, simple, yet firm yes.

Wesley took a moment to regard her skeptically before Jason disrupted his stare.

"Well, I'm glad Mama is not here all by herself," remarked Jason.

"Mama, why didn't you tell us you had someone helping you?" asked Wesley, still trying to wrap his mind around this woman.

"Oh…I forgot...I mean…well….it just slipped my mind. But it's nothing to fret about."

Mama's explanation was as simple as that, and Wesley and Jason could do nothing else but accept it. Mama sent the boys off to settle into their room and get ready for dinner. As he unpacked, Jason felt a bit nostalgic as he looked around the small room. Mama had been living in Miracle Village ever since its establishment after the earthquake in 2010. The missionaries who built the town offered rent-free living to amputees first, and then to others that had been severely affected by the earthquake. Mama was definitely in need having lost everything she had in the disaster. It left her homeless and hopeless. So finding refuge in Miracle Village brought about unspeakable gratitude within her. However, her current accommodations were a far cry from the lavish life her husband had provided, but she decided that she could more than make do here.

The house was small, but she was able to petition the missionaries to allow her to extend her little home in order to better accommodate her growing boys. They typically did not permit any modifications to the structures, but they accepted Mama's rationale. She in turn added another bedroom, a larger living area, and a quaint dining space. The additions ended up making the home almost twice as large as its original intent. Mama knew this would be a big change for the boys. Compared to their old life, this was nothing they were accustomed to, but she tried her best to make the house as nice as their old home. Little did Mama know, all the luxuries paled in comparison to the joy they felt just being near her.

As always, Mama's only concern was that her boys were well taken care of. They were young at the time of the earthquake and thankfully, they weren't even in Haiti when it happened. They had been staying with their aunt in the U.S. attending school. Their father insisted that they received an American education. He often repeated, "Only the best private schools for my boys." There was a routine in place; they would go to school abroad during the academic year and return to

Haiti to spend their summers here with Mama. By the time January 12th came around, the boys were back in New York City attending their winter classes safe from harm.

By now, the boys had outgrown their old bedroom, but it was clear that not one thing about the room had changed. Mama had kept it exactly the same and spotless as always. As Jason looked around, memories of him and his brother getting into all types of trouble ran through his mind. Truth be told, Jason was the one that used to get into the most trouble although he would never admit it. Though he was the younger of the two, Mama always held him accountable. In reality, he always knew he deserved every punishment, as he was often the one to drag Wesley into his mischief. Wesley, often the more cautious of the two, would follow only to protect his baby brother. He would usually take part in the mischief, inadvertently of course, landing them both in hot water with Mama.

Jason's eyes darted around the small bedroom as his mind conjured up images of him and his brother fooling around and play-fighting in the tiny space. He smiled as he remembered how some of those fights quickly became real. He could almost see ghostly shadows of him and his brother swinging their limbs in an effort to tear each other apart. But they often only made a mess of their room. He stood up from the bed and moved toward the wall where he shifted an old picture that hung on an old rusted nail, and yep, that hole in the wall was still there. Jason chuckled to himself. That happened when he accidentally kicked into the wall when he and Wesley were play fighting one day. He remembered placing the picture there to hide the hole from Mama, and to his pleasant surprise, she never found out.

Wesley barging back into the room snapped Jason out of his reverie.

"Hey bro, what you think about Mama's nurse?" asked Wesley as he plopped down on his old creaky bed.

"I don't know man," Jason shrugged him off.

"Well I don't like her," said Wesley.

"But you just met her; she didn't even say two words yet."

"Yeah, and you already love her."

Jason rolled his eyes at his brother's dramatics.

"I saw the way you were looking at her when she opened the door," Wesley mocked googly eyes. Jason laughed and threw a pillow his way, but Wesley quickly dodged it.

"I just feel a strange energy from her. There's something special about her," Jason finally replied.

"Yeah I feel it too, and I don't like it."

"Well, I'm curious."

"Suit yourself baby bro. In the meantime, I'm gonna go help Mama set the table for dinner."

With that, Wesley was out the door and Jason soon followed after. Once they parted the beaded drape that led into the kitchen, they both abruptly stopped, surprised to see Detra at the dinner table.

"You're still here?" asked Wesley, annoyed.

"Yes," she responded, "I am to stay here at all times."

"Is that so?" asked Jason, now intrigued. If she was staying here, that meant that he could go ahead and feed his curiosity.

Wesley however, perturbed by the news, was under the impression that Detra only spent a couple of hours out of the day with Mama. He had no idea that she was practically living there, and the thought made him uncomfortable for several reasons. The first being he did not like the idea that his mother needed someone. In his mind, Mama was perfectly healthy and did not need additional help around the house. Secondly, if she did need help, it should not come from a stranger, especially someone as strange as Detra. He immediately picked up an oddity from her, and he did not like it.

Mama finished setting the table and sat down. The table packed with food, displayed all the boys'

favorites. The special tonight was *lambi ak diri,*
conch and rice. It was a feast fit for ten, but Mama
knew that her two sons would inhale it all in a
heartbeat.

"Well, I'm glad that my babies are here, so let's start
this meal with a prayer. Detra would you do us the
honor please?"

Detra turned to look at Mama, a bit surprised by her
request, "Yes sure. Close your eyes and bow your
head everyone as we go before The Master. God of
Life and Death, please bless this meal. Amen."

Wesley nudged Jason giving him a confused look.
Jason read him and knew he was wondering what the
hell was wrong with this girl.

As they began sharing the food, Wesley noticed that
Detra's plate was empty. He figured she would serve
herself later. The room was silent for a while, the only
interruption being the clink and clatter of utensils.
The boys were focused on their food and they made
sure to savor every bite, as they knew this kind of
food was not readily available to them while away at
school. No other cuisine compared, especially not the
food served on campus. Mama's cooking was
considered a delicacy to them. When Wesley finally
looked up from his plate, ready for a second round, he
noticed that Detra had still yet to eat anything.

"You're not eating?" he asked her.

"No. I'm not hungry." Her voice came out ice cold, disinterested, and disengaged, and it annoyed Wesley.

She was as stiff as a rock. Not moving a muscle, barely blinking.

"You know what, for a nurse, you're not very warm. I thought nurses were supposed to be nice," said Wesley.

Detra smiled a little, the first sign of emotion she'd shown all night, "Actually, I'm very nice."

"I don't see it," retaliated Wesley, "Mama, does she treat you good? Because I don't want anyone staying with you that treats you bad."

"Wesley, stop," warned his mother.

"But Mama, I don't understand her. You said you know her from church, but I just can't see it. She doesn't seem like a church girl to me," Wesley, notably agitated by this woman's presence could feel something was not quite right. It was disturbing, and it gave him goose bumps.

"Wesley why are you so upset?" Detra asked him, tautly.

"And why do you talk like that? Mama where did you find this woman?" he said turning back to his mother.

"You do not know who I am," Detra calmly spoke again.

"Exactly! Who the hell are you!?"

Detra responded with a simple smile to herself.

As they went back and forth, Jason just sat back and watched their banter like a television special. It intrigued him how Detra never really said much and the less she said the more upset Wesley got. He wondered why Wesley was so agitated by her. He thought to himself that Wesley was right; there was definitely something about this girl. The two just had very different reactions to her. While Wesley could hardly stand the sight of her, Jason wanted to find out more about her. It was peculiar how quickly they both felt strong but opposite emotions towards Detra. This storm of a woman. Quiet but powerful.

"Wesley stop, just stop," Mama finally said, "I know you don't get it, but Detra has actually helped me out a lot."

"Of course I don't get it; I just came here and found a bizarre woman living with my mother. You never told us about her. Why? If you needed help, we could have been here for you. No need to bring an outsider in your house Mama."

In fact, Wesley had offered Mama to come live in The U.S. with them. He did not like that she decided to stay back on the island alone.

However, Mama was stubborn, and she wanted to stay in Haiti. She was born here, and she wanted to live and die here. Buried too.

"Wesley, Detra has helped me in ways you just can't understand for now," Mama replied.

"Tell me!" he begged.

At this moment, Detra silently got up and left the table.

"You see? You made her leave," reproached Jason.

"I don't care."

"Wesley, you were raised better than this. Respect our guest." Mama stood up and glared at Wesley, "Trust me, you don't wanna mess with her, so please, for me my baby, please just stop."

With that, Mama stood up and decided to retire to her room, leaving the cleanup work to the boys. She was glad to have her sons home, but she knew that things would not be peaceful or quiet with them around. It never was. Growing up, the boys definitely caused Mama some memorable headaches. The brothers were always bickering and going back and forth with one another. They fought ferociously, quarreled endlessly, and they rarely saw eye to eye on anything. It was more than obvious that not much had changed over the years.

They have been this way since they were small, and they would more than likely stay that way. More than anything though, Mama knew that no matter how much they fought, her sons loved each other deeply. Their brotherhood was tight and their bond unmatched. Though they may be at each other's throats one minute, they would be making up that very next minute. The younger looked up to the older and the older protected the younger. It was the healthiest of cycles.

They were close, so close that they secretly could not spend too much time apart. When Wesley left home to attend college, Jason was hot on his trail that next year to attend the same school. Wesley went pre-law while Jason went pre-med. The two were inseparable, and Mama could not be prouder. One son to be a lawyer and the other to be a doctor. It was a dream come true for any mother. She just prayed that nothing would ever separate the two.

While Mama rested, the brothers got busy putting the kitchen back together. Soon after, they went their separate ways. Wesley went to the bedroom while Jason found himself wandering around the little house, taking everything in. He took note of any changes made to the small space within the last year. Everything looked the same, as always. If Mama was anything, she was predictable, but her predictability provided him with a sense of stability.

From the black and white checkered kitchen tablecloth, to the old wooden wall clock hanging in the living room, nothing altered. The only difference being a brand new silver picture frame they gifted her for Christmas last year. The frame held a picture of Mama and the boys when they were just babies. Jason picked it up and stared for a bit. Mama looked so beautiful in the old photograph, but she was still beautiful now of course. Her smile almost as wide as the frame itself and her eyes full of hope and love. Her eyes looked the same still, except a little bit less hope, and definitely a lot more love. He smiled to himself and put the frame down before continuing his journey throughout the house. It felt good to be here.

Jason always loved coming to see Mama, and he and Wesley made sure to do so at least once a year. Jason hated that she lived alone, and he worried for her as she grew older. He wanted to make sure she would be well taken care of. The money he sent to her from time to time was helpful, but he knew it would not compare to his actual presence. Unlike Wesley, Jason was actually glad that Mama had someone staying here with her, but still he was curious about exactly who this person was.

Jason kept walking through the house when something caught his attention. In the corner of his eye, he saw a white sheet floating in the wind out on the veranda. As he approached the exit leading outside, he realized that it was Detra standing out, looking up at the night sky.

He watched her lean against the metal railing, her white dress and dark hair flowing behind her in the wind. He could not understand why he was so mesmerized by this woman. She had only uttered but two words to him, and yet she had already captured him, and in some way, Wesley too.

"Why are you watching me Jason?"

Jason was surprised. He thought he was being discreet. Apparently not. He stood at the doorway as he responded.

"How did you know I was here?"

She turned around, leaned against the railing and crossed her arms across her chest, "I felt you."

"You felt me? How?"

"Instinct."

There was a moment of silence between the two. The loud chirping of the crickets was the only sound filling the space. Jason approached Detra and joined her by the railing.

"What are you doing out here?" he asked her.

"Talking to God."

Jason smiled at how churchy she sounded. Guess she wasn't lying when she said she knew Mama from church. "You mean the stars? The moon?" he asked.

Jason loved the island mostly for the simple fact that the stars were the most visible out here. Out of all the traveling he did, nothing compared to the night sky of his childhood island. He absolutely understood how Detra could be looking for God out here.

"I meant what I said," she replied.

Her sharp answer did not deter him.

"So you talk to God?" he asked skeptically.

"Yes."

"And He talks back?" he asked quizzically.

"Sometimes. He likes to show more than talk. He's a being of few words actually," she smiled.

Jason could not help but to smile back. She was so beautiful, a rare kind of beauty. He had never encountered anyone that looked like her. Nor had he felt anything like her before.

"So what is He saying?"

"He's telling me to remember who I am."

"And who is that?"

"I am Detra."

"Ok," he frowned at her stating the obvious, "well Detra, are you from around here? I find that you speak English very well."

"I'm from everywhere. And I speak many languages."

Jason continued to pry. "So you travel a lot, I take it."

"You could say that."

Detra's responses were vague and left him dissatisfied, however, Jason continued conversing. "You're so elusive. I think that's why my brother is so disturbed by you."

"Disturbed?" she asked. "He's not just disturbed; your brother clearly doesn't like me at all. I know. But I'm not surprised, most people don't."

"Why not?"

"I take it they're afraid of me."

"Should they be?"

"Are you?"

Detra turned to look him straight in the eyes. He stared back at her and swallowed hard. She was something else, and he could not quite put his finger on it.

"No," he answered truthfully.

He saw a look of surprise cross her features. It was the most emotion he had seen her express since they met, however it was short lived as she quickly masked it. The wind blew, almost violently, and her hair took over her face while her white dress flapped against her legs.

"I think it's time for this conversation to be over," she stated.

Jason was far from finished with the conversation and he tried to keep talking to her. "Why? Are you going to sleep?"

"I don't sleep much."

"Me neither," agreed Jason attempting to find common ground with her.

"You need it though. You need rest Jason."

"They say sleep is the cousin of death," Jason stated. It's something he's heard people say in passing.

Detra laughed. It was the first time Jason heard such a sound.

"More like second cousin," she said, "twice removed."

Jason found himself laughing too. He wasn't sure why, but he found that amusing. More than just that, he found her laugh contagious.

"Jason baby, go to bed," his mother's voice resonated from behind him, startling him. She had woken up from her nap, and she wanted to come out and catch some fresh air.

Jason turned around and quickly obeyed, "Yes Mama," he paused to kiss her on her cheek before heading in.

Mama approached Detra and held on to the railing, "Thank you again, for everything," said Mama.

"Thank Him."

Mama paused a moment and watched Detra as she stared up into the night sky.

"I'm sorry for Wesley's behavior earlier."

"Don't worry about it. It doesn't change anything." Detra turned to look at Mama, "Your sons, they sense me."

"Yeah, my babies, they've always been very intuitive."

"They're special. Both of them," Detra
acknowledged.

"I know."

Mama took in a deep breath before speaking, "Let me
know if you need anything."

"I don't."

Mama turned to go back inside the house and left
Detra to the sky.

Chapter Two

Summer nights on the island were beyond brutal. The heat was unbearable, and the mosquitoes were vicious. This was something that Jason had almost forgotten. But after opening up the bedroom window to let some fresh air in and making sure to saturate his body with mosquito repellant, Jason was finally able to doze off.

The night passed quickly and soon the sun beamed through the windows, illuminating the entire space. Jason slowly peeled his eyes open as they adjusted to the morning glare. He felt a ferocious growl in his stomach and knew that it was time for breakfast. Wiping the sleep from his eyes, he got up in search of food leaving his brother still dreaming.

He padded barefoot across the floors towards the kitchen and to his dismay he found that the pantry was empty. With that, he grabbed an apple out of the fruit bowl and went to get dressed; he figured he would just go to the market place to buy something to eat.

Jason was astonished that Mama was not up yet. Mama was known to be an early riser, usually up and at 'em by the break of dawn. Jason peeked into her room to check on her, but it seemed as though she was still fast asleep. He was about to get Wesley to accompany him while he took care of the groceries, when he caught sight of Detra sitting out on the veranda. He paused to take a look at her.

"Why are you watching me Jason?"

Jason chuckled to himself. There goes that "instinct" thing again, he thought.

"You spent the night out here?" he asked her, ignoring her question.

"Yes, I did."

Odd. He wondered how she was able to deal with the constant mosquito attacks.

He approached her and watched as her eyes scanned his body. He had almost forgotten that he was only wearing a pair of boxers.

His lean caramel torso was exposed and now tingling from her stare. Though there seemed to be no desire in her eyes, he was still surprised by her unabashed gaze.

"Well, I'm on my way to the market place, would you like to come with me?" Jason figured he ought to extend an invitation to her instead of his brother. Knowing Wesley, he would rather sleep through the morning anyway.

"I don't think that's a good idea," she replied apprehensively.

"Why not? Mama needs groceries, you're here to help, so help," he challenged.

A small smile played on the corners of her lips, "Do you really want me to come Jason?"

"I meant what I said."

She admittedly liked his answer.

Jason got dressed and then met Detra by the door to head out. It happened to be a peculiarly windy day that day, so both Detra and Jason's hair were flowing in the wind like wild manes as they walked.

The market place was a good distance from the village. The villagers would have to trek almost an hour to buy groceries, and return carrying the heavy loads.

Even though the missionaries built a marketplace next to the village to solve the issue, vendors were not willing to take the journey all the way out there to sell their goods, so the trip to the city was always inevitable. This was one of the challenges of living in Miracle Village.

Almost the entire way there, Detra kept quiet, which made Jason a little bit uncomfortable. Yet Jason shrugged it off and they continued their travels in silence.

It was a busy morning in the market place with customers loudly bartering with the vendors as they made their purchases. All the while, in the midst of the chaos, the intense silence between Detra and Jason remained. The pair kept walking as Jason absentmindedly picked fruit from the various stands they were passing. Abruptly, he stopped and grabbed a bunch of *keneps* from one of the stands.

"Oooh, I love kenep! It's been so long since I've had one!" he exclaimed.

Keneps were the boys' favorite fruit ever since they were young. They often stole them from their neighbor's yard when they were younger growing up on the island. Their neighbor would complain to Mama and she would spank them to keep them from stealing again. But that never stopped them, Wesley and Jason always took the discipline in stride. To them, it was all worth it for that sweet taste of kenep. Jason could only ever get his hands on them while he was in Haiti. They were almost impossible to find abroad. And even if he could find keneps elsewhere, he was convinced that they would never taste as sweet as they did in Haiti.

"How do they taste?" asked Detra, with a hint of curiosity in her eyes.

Jason's eyes widened in shock, "Don't tell me you never tried one?"

Detra gently shook her head no.

"How is it that you live here and never had kenep? You have to try one."

"How?"

"How what?" Jason's eyebrows furrowed, "How do you eat it?" he asked clarifying.

She just nodded her head yes.

"Here, I'll show you."

Jason bought a batch of keneps from the vendor and immediately popped one of the small fruits off the bunch. He bit into it cracking the fragile skin and licked the seed out. He sucked on the seed for a while before spitting it out into a napkin.

"You see, it's simple and easy."

He handed Detra a kenep and watched as she eyed the fruit suspiciously. Jason playfully rolled his eyes at her hesitancy, he took the fruit from her hand and put it up to her mouth. He nodded as if to tell her to go ahead and bite into it. He watched her as she sucked the seed into her lips. Jason looked on mesmerized by how her expression brightened immediately. She closed her eyes and relished in the juices now dancing on her tongue. She opened her eyes to find Jason staring at her.

"You have to spit the seed out now."

"I can't eat it?" she mumbled through a mouthful.

"No, if you eat it, you'll die," he joked.

She laughed. That was the second time Jason heard that sound and once again, he was absorbed by it. Opening the napkin, he let her spit the seed out, and then watched her lick the remainder of the fruit juices off her full lips. Jason was entranced.

"I want more," she stated.

"Anything you want."

He gave her some more keneps to snack on as they continued their walk through the market place. Jason was stunned again when Detra revealed that she had never had sugar cane.

He made her try some and again watched in awe as she enjoyed her first taste of sugar cane. He laughed a little as he watched her try to chew down the cane residue. He told her that she had to spit that out too.

"So you like it?" he asked.

"Love," she quirked her eyebrow and nodded her head. "I think this is love."

He smiled at how she said the word as if it were a foreign term. "What does it taste like?" he asked her.

"It tastes like heaven."

"You want more?"

"Yes." She quickly responded.

Before she could indulge in another bite, an elderly woman stopped and addressed her.

"*Sa wap fe la*?" What are you doing here? the woman asked her.

Jason observed as the two exchanged an extensive stare. The older woman had a full head of grey hair, she was hunched over and holding on to a cane intricately carved out of wood. Her skin was as tough as leather and it noticeably sagged off her high cheekbones. Her eyes were dark pools filled with a knowing. Jason looked on as they continued their conversation in a language that he did not quite understand, Haitian Creole; the language the natives of the island spoke. Although Jason was a native, he never really fully grasped the dialect.

"*Map fe yon comision.*" I'm running an errand, Detra answered the old woman.

"*Fre'm te dim li te we'w yer swa.*" My brother told me he saw you last night, retorted the old woman.

"*Mwen kon sa.*" Yes, I know.

"*Li di'm ou te fe'l pe, pou tet sa, li couri, l'ale nan Jacmel.*" He said you scared him, so he ran off to the town of Jacmel, the woman continued.

"*Min se li me'm ki fe'm sezi. Mwen te sezi we'l la paske mwen gen rendezvous avek li nan Jacmel aswe'a.*" Actually, I was the one surprised to see him here since I have an appointment with him tonight in Jacmel, said Detra.

"*Mwen te di'l pa couri,*" I told him not to run; a shadow of worry took over the old woman's wrinkly face.

"*Pa inkyete'w cheri, tout bagay pral bien pase.*" Don't worry dear, everything is going to be well, Detra said in a soft voice.

"*Ou promet?*" You promise.

"*Promet.*" Promise, Detra finally said.

With that, the old woman walked off but before she did so, she gave Jason a look of pity that left him perplexed.

"What was that all about?" asked Jason.

"She was asking me about her brother."

"And you know her brother?"

"Yes I do."

Jason could tell by her tone that she was not willing to talk much more about this subject. Detra became stoic again. Rigid almost, and it caught Jason off guard. Jason was dumbfounded by how quickly Detra returned to her austere demeanor. Just about a minute ago, they were laughing and enjoying new fruit, and now she was back to the icy woman he first encountered. Jason questioned what her and that old woman had discussed to make her retreat so abruptly.

"Let's go back home to your mother now," she announced.

She did not give Jason a moment to protest the notion as they were quickly on their way back to the village. Jason wondered why she was all of a sudden in such a hurry to get home. Racing back to Miracle Village, Detra seemed to be floating ahead of him while Jason lagged behind trying his best to catch up.

He tried to fight off the sun's glare by using his handkerchief to wipe off his sweat that was now flowing like a faucet. It was close to noon and the sun was relentless, brutal even, and its rays were personally attacking Jason. At least that's what he felt was happening. However, it appeared as if Detra was not affected by the burning sun at all. She had yet to shed a bead of sweat. Once they finally reached the house, Jason found an upset Wesley pacing around outside on the veranda.

"Jason, where were you?" asked Wesley. Jason could sense the alarm in his voice.

"I went to the market place to get some groceries for Mama," he said lifting the shopping bags up as evidence, "what's wrong bro?"

Wesley glared at Detra, "Well while you were out with her," he cut his eyes at Detra, "I was here trying to take care of Mama. She's not feeling good."

Jason's eyes pained with worry, "Where is she?"

"She's inside, lying down in her room."

As he was about to rush in to go see her, he felt Detra swiftly hurry past him towards Mama's room. Without a word, she entered Mama's room and closed the door behind her.

Once she was out of earshot Wesley spoke, "What is she going to do?"

"I don't know man; she said she's the nurse, so maybe she knows how to help."

"Well I hope so. Maybe she will be good for something around here. She claims she is here to help, but I have yet to see her do anything. Mama does everything, the cooking, the cleaning, the whole lot! I'm sure she didn't help Mama cook yesterday, and she sure as hell did not help us clean the kitchen afterwards. She even left Mama alone this morning, what is she even doing here?"

Jason ignored Wesley's rant, "What's wrong with Mama?" he was more concerned about their mother.

"I don't know. I went to see her when I woke up this morning and she told me she had a headache and she felt weak and a bit dizzy. She didn't even have enough strength to get out of bed. I've never seen her like this."

The boys had never seen their Mama sick. She has always been as strong as an ox. Wesley hated seeing her so weak this morning; he was worried, and he felt helpless.

"I asked if she wanted me to take her to the hospital," he continued, "but she said that she would just wait for Detra to come back."

Right on cue, Mama's bedroom door swung open and she stepped out with a pep in her step. Wesley looked at her surprised; this was a total one eighty change from how she was feeling this morning.

"Mama, how are you feeling?" asked Jason as he approached her with his arms out, ready for one of her legendary embraces.

"Oh baby, I'm good," she replied, pulling him to her chest and hugging him back.

"Wesley told me you were sick."

"Well, I didn't feel so good this morning, but I'm all better now."

"Are you sure Mama?" asked Wesley, the panic still lingering in his voice.

"Yeah baby, no need to worry."

Detra stepped out of the bedroom and all eyes were on her. She abruptly stopped walking before turning around to leave again. Wesley's voice stopped her in her tracks.

"I don't know what you did but thank you for helping my Mama."

Detra acknowledged Wesley with a simple nod. Before he could say anything further, she had already smoothly slipped out of the house.

Chapter Three

Evening fell upon the little island like a blanket. The neighborhood was dark, quaint and quiet, with the exception of Mama's house. Mama's was the only house in Miracle Village still emanating light. The home was filled with the melodic sounds of laughter and music. Wesley and Jason were singing and dancing in front of their mother; putting on their own little variety show. Mama, amused beyond measure, fell back against the couch in laughter as she watched their silly antics. She even joined in amusingly attempting some of the latest dance moves and surprisingly enough, kept up with them. Mama flipped the script as well and showed them some moves from back in her day. After wiping her tears of laughter, Mama asked Jason to play his old guitar.

"Oh Mama, you know I don't play anymore," Jason protested.

"For me please baby," Mama, asked lovingly.

Playing the guitar brought up a number of unresolved issues within Jason. When he was younger, Jason used to love to play the guitar. He even considered a career in music at one time. But before his father passed away, he ordered him to pursue a real career. There were not many positive things that could be said about the boys' father. He was never the most compassionate of their parents, but one thing was for sure; he was an excellent provider. Before sickness had befallen him, their father sat the boys down and told them that they would soon be the men of the house. He then instructed them to take care of their Mama. Jason and Wesley took their father's word to heart by pursuing careers that met their father's standards. For that reason, Jason put his musical dreams aside. It was years since Jason picked up his guitar. Now Mama was asking him to play, and how could he ever deny his queen.

Jason dusted off his old guitar. He found it in the same corner where she always kept it. It was one of the few things Mama was able to salvage from the earthquake aftermath. Through the rubble, the guitar somehow remained intact. Mama called it a miracle. Jason started lightly fingering the familiar chords. An old melody then slowly crept through his spine and manifested into his fingertips.

He had played the familiar melody when he was younger. He wished he could say he composed it, but he could not. He always felt like someone else composed it and dropped it into his mind somehow. Though there were no words to the song, the tune told a story of love. Perhaps love for his mother. Maybe for a woman in his life. Or possibly just his love for music. The sounds of the guitar strings filled the entire house and it elevated the atmosphere. Aside from Jason's guitar playing, there was complete silence. Not even the crickets were chirping. Every living thing within earshot locked into this song.

When he finished playing, Jason looked up to catch Detra standing by the door staring straight at him. Mama and Wesley had their backs to her, so Jason was the only one able to see her. For some reason, Jason felt like he was the only one who would have been able to see her in this moment. It was bizarre. Their eyes met and locked. She did not blink; she did not waver, and never shied away. She stood there watching, gradually releasing a breath. Her eyes were wide with wonderment and Jason could not help but to smile to himself. While Mama and Wesley were completely oblivious to what was happening, Jason could not seem to pull away from her eyes. That was until his concentration was broken by his mother's joyous applause.

"That was beautiful baby," Mama exclaimed. He bent down to kiss her cheek before continuing his theatrics with his brother.

Wesley and Jason spent some more time entertaining Mama with a couple more stories from their lives in America. They comically re-enacted scenarios, and Mama laughed uncontrollably at her silly boys. It was not very long after, Mama retired to her room to get some rest. Wesley had wandered off somewhere, which left Jason time to himself.

He decided to go in search of Detra. Not having to search long, he found her sitting on the back porch stairs. The moon shone brightly that night and it gave everything around a light blue tint, including Detra's beautiful, flawless skin. Jason watched her for a little before he stepped out to join her on the stairs.

"Talking to God again?" he asked.

"Always," she replied.

Jason took a moment to gaze at her. Detra sat with her back straightened, feet planted, looking straight ahead. She was motionless with the exception of her hair rustling in the wind. Jason knowingly stared at her, but he knew he had to say something before the silence became awkward.

"I see you were watching me earlier," he stated, now flipping Detra's previous inquiry on her.

She turned to face him, "Your music is heavenly Jason; you play like an angel."

Jason blushed. He used to receive all sorts of compliments on his playing before, but it felt different coming from her.

"And you just happen to know what an angel sounds like?"

"Yes," she smiled, "like you."

Her smile had caught him off guard and he found himself relishing in it.

A moment passed between them before she continued, "You have a very special gift from God. That song you were playing, it came from Him."

Jason was in awe. He did not know what to say. He just sat and listened. He wasn't quite sure why, but he felt that he couldn't speak while she spoke, out of reverence for her.

"You may not understand now, but you will see one day how powerful you and your brother really are. You are a healer Jason. That music you played, it's not just soothing, it actually heals. It repairs wounds, it undoes damage."

Jason swallowed hard; he could not believe what he was hearing. Somehow, instinctively, he knew what she was saying was true. He thought that maybe this woman was a psychic or a spiritual advisor.

She knew things that others would never know. In that moment, Jason knew Detra heard from God. She spoke to Him and He spoke back to her. Jason decided to continue probing.

"And my brother?" he questioned.

"Your brother is a defender of persons. He speaks for the unspoken. He rights wrongs," she replied.

Her response made a lot of sense to Jason. He was astounded at how much she already knew about them.

"The two of you are strong individually," she continued, "but together you are a force. Nothing will come between the two of you. Not even me."

"How would you come between us?"

"I've already said too much," Detra replied in reluctance.

"Is it because he doesn't like you and I do?"

She smiled again, but it didn't reach her eyes, "you like me Jason?"

He just shrugged and leaned back against his elbows.

"I think you're just drawn to me," she said.

"Perhaps," he said, "but what's sure is that I need to know more about who you are."

Detra turned back to look straight ahead, "Why so curious?"

He just shrugged.

"Curiosity isn't always a good thing Jason."

"You know so much, and I just need to know how. There is definitely something about you. Who are you?"

She turned her head to look at him, "I already told you, I'm Detra."

"Yeah, but there's something more. There's something different." He came back up to look her in her eyes, "Yesterday, how did you help my Mama? What did you do to her?"

"I just helped her feel better."

"You have healing powers?" he prodded.

"I'm able to help people feel better for a moment. Healing belongs to God."

"Is that why Mama keeps you around?"

Detra remained silent, which pushed Jason to prompt more answers from her.

"Detra, is my Mama sick?"

She heard the worry in his voice and she wished she could do something about it, but she was powerless in that sense.

"Jason, your mother is going to be okay," replied Detra.

That answer did nothing to subdue Jason's worries, but he decided to leave the topic alone for now. He whipped his shoes off and dug his bare feet into the grass beneath him. Detra's eyebrows furrowed as she took in his actions.

"What are you doing?" she asked.

"Playing in the grass with my toes."

"Why?"

Jason simply responded, "Because it feels good."

He abruptly got up and grabbed her ankle. Detra flinched at the initial contact, but then she was surprised that he seemed unbothered by the touch. He gently removed each of her slippers and placed her feet in the grass.

"Oh. This feels good," Detra was amazed to feel the contrast of the hot temperature and the coolness of the grass against her feet.

"Wiggle your toes," he instructed her.

She did as he said, then she started to run her feet back and forth against the grass. Each blade caressed the soles of her feet and tickled the spaces in between her toes. She smiled.

"Feels nice right?" he asked.

"Yes it does."

"You've never done this before?" Jason inquired.

He wondered how is it that a girl from the island had never felt grass against her feet before. Strange to say the least.

"No, I've never tried it before."

Jason watched as Detra threw her head back and let out a moan of pleasure that resonated through him. Her eyes closed and the moon shining on her skin made her look like the most radiant being on Earth. He could have stayed there and watched her for hours, instead, he found himself running into the house returning with a coconut. Detra mentioned earlier that she never tried one, and of course, he wanted to be the one to introduce her to this island delicacy. Jason even took the trek all the way back to the market earlier that day just to pick out the right first coconut for her. After slicing the top open with a machete, he held the coconut to her lips and watched as she swallowed the water.

Her throat moved up and down and with each gulp, Jason became hypnotized. Some of the water spilled down her chin and Jason's eyes followed the trail down her collarbone and then further into her blouse. He slowly lowered the coconut down and watched her lips twitch into a small smile.

"Good?" he asked.

"Yes," she whispered as she touched her lips with her fingertips.

A woman, who had never tasted kenep, sugar cane, or coconut; who has never felt grass beneath her toes and had healing powers. Jason figured that Detra was not from around here. Perhaps she was from another world; but for some reason, Jason was not scared. He lifted the coconut up to his mouth to take a drink and found that his lips now tingled with a warmth. It confirmed what he already sensed; Detra was indeed special.

"Jason, you've shown me so much," Detra told him.

"I want to show you more."

She blinked and shied away a little, "I think you've already done enough."

Jason scooted a little closer to her, "Why don't you know about any of this? Where are you from?"

His questions were saturated in curiosity. They dripped of wonder, and he had the burning desire to know more about her.

Before Detra could answer his questions, both their heads snapped up at the sound of a voice.

"*Ou la toujou?*" You're still here? The voice of the same elderly woman from the market place resonated. She was walking up the path and had stopped in front of the porch.

"*Mwen poko fini ak commision an.*" Still running errands, Detra replied.

"*Et fre'm?*" And my brother, the old woman questioned.

What was meant to be has happened. "*Sak te gen pou fet gintan fet,*" Detra answered.

"*Tout bagay bien pase?*" Everything went well, asked the woman.

Yes, as promised, "*Oui, mwen te promet ou.*" Detra's voice was calm as she reassured the woman.

And me, when will be my day? "*Et mwen mem? Ki le kap tou pam,*" the old woman inquired.

Detra's voice spoke peace. Patience my child. "*Pacience pitit mwen.*"

"*Pa blie'm*." Do not forget me.

"*Jamais.*" Never, reassured Detra.

The exchange ended, and the old woman continued on her way. Detra looked over to see Jason watching her. She knew he was curious to know about their conversation.

"What did she want?" he asked.

"She wanted to know about her brother."

"Is he okay?"

"He died."

Jason gasped, "Oh no. You weren't able to heal him?"

"It was his time."

A gust of wind blew again, this time rustling the leaves in the nearby trees. Without a word, Detra stood up to head inside the house. Before leaving, she turned back to Jason and firmly said, "Death also belongs to God."

Chapter Four

"So she's a healer?" Wesley asked, his eyebrow raised in skepticism.

Jason had just told him everything that he knew so far about Detra, including their strange encounter with the elderly woman.

"Yeah, I think that's why Mama has her staying here," replied Jason.

"You think something's wrong with Mama?" Wesley questioned.

"If there is, you know she would never tell us."

"Yeah, she doesn't want us to worry," agreed Wesley.

"You're still not fond of Detra are you?" asked Jason, "Even though she's here to help? And now you see exactly how she helps."

Jason thought that telling Wesley everything about Detra would ease his dislike for her. However, Wesley's reaction was exactly the opposite of what Jason had hoped. Knowing more about Detra only heightened Wesley's anxiety. Initially, he sensed that Detra was bizarre, but now, he knew for a fact that she was. If Detra was a healer, he wondered what ailed his mother. And if Detra was not able to heal that old woman's brother, he feared that chances were she would not be able to heal his mother either.

The boys had seen their father's health deplete right before their eyes. They were only nine and ten years old at the time of their father's death. They were spending the summer in Haiti and prior to their arrival, word had gotten to them that their father was sick. They did not realize the severity of the situation until they saw him face to face. His eyes were dark and sunken in. His skin, once clear, bright and shiny was now pale, dry, and plagued with scabbing. His once strong, tall, muscular build had diminished to a hunched over skeletal shell of a body. He was a far cry from the stern forty-something year old dad they left behind. It was only the previous year they left to attend school abroad with their aunt. Jason and Wesley could never forget the experience of leaving their father a healthy man one summer only to return to a dying man the following year. The doctors said it was cancer, and that there was nothing to be done, not at this stage.

Their last memory of that summer was attending their father's funeral. Their worst nightmare would be to relive the same experience with the only parent they had left. It would be harder this time. Their bond with Mama was something they both cherished. Unlike their mother, their father was a cold man. They never developed a father-son relationship with him, but they loved him all the same. It was tough watching him go but losing their Mama in the same way would destroy them. It was their biggest fear and a pain they would never get through.

Mama had always been as strong as an ox. Not once in their whole lives could they remember her having an ailment, nor a malady that could stop her. Her main purpose was to protect her children, provide, and take care of the house. Whether it was making sure they were in school, keeping them well fed and healthy, or instilling discipline, Mama stopped at nothing to make sure her children were cared for. Ever since their father passed, Mama carried the family on her back, and perhaps, things had started to catch up with her. Now that the boys were older, the roles had reversed. It was now their mission to take care of Mama, but they were afraid that it might be too late. They felt helpless; when Mama is sick, everyone is sick.

"I don't know man," said Wesley letting out an exaggerated breath, "I'm still not completely comfortable with her."

Wesley plopped down on his old bed. "Why are you so comfortable with her?" he questioned Jason. "Doesn't she creep you out too?"

The vibe Wesley got when Detra came around told him to run in the opposite direction. Yet here was Jason actually running towards her, chasing her even. They did not always agree on everything, but Wesley felt so discordant with his brother when it came to Detra. He knew nothing could ever come between them, but now, it felt like they were heading in different directions and he did not like it.

"Well, for starters there are a lot of things about her I feel the need to know," Jason replied. "She said some beautiful things about us last night. Things I have never heard anyone say. And when she spoke, I felt like she was so sure of everything. There was no trace of doubt in her eyes. She speaks absolute truth."

"You like her," Wesley said as he waived off everything Jason said. Wesley reduced Jason's words to nothing more than a schoolboy's crush.

"I'm attracted to her," Jason admitted. "There's something about her that draws me in."

Wesley looked up to see his brother deeply lost in his thoughts. He wondered how Jason became so enthralled by this woman. Yes, she was beautiful; even he had to admit that she was one of the most beautiful women he had ever seen.

Her beauty was rare, unearthly even and perhaps that was what his brother was drawn to. Yet Wesley still wondered how could Jason not see past her beauty and detect that there was something very peculiar about her. Then again, maybe he did detect it, and that was the very reason why he felt the need to get close to her. While Wesley was the prudent one, Jason was the thrill seeker and it could be that his latest brush with adrenaline had a name, Detra.

Wesley recalled an experience they had when they were kids spending the summer on the island. He remembered that their neighbor had an ox, a massive ox used to carry heavy loads and also used for ground cultivation. Its head was adorned with the most ominous, sharpest set of horns any ox could possess. It was ferocious and feared but Jason was never intimidated. Though Wesley often warned Jason to stay away from the ox, Jason would still approach it and even sit on it. He would sometimes pull out his guitar to try to charm the beast with his music. To Wesley's surprise, the ox never resisted. Jason would try to convince Wesley to pet the ox, but Wesley dare not go near it. He knew what the ox was capable of doing. He knew its strength and its capability to turn on you at any moment, and because of that he stayed away.

One day, while Jason straddled the ox, the creature flared and bucked, throwing Jason ten feet up in the air and tossing him to the ground. Thankfully, Jason was able to quickly get up and outrun the animal when it charged at him.

Lucky for him, he got away with just a few scrapes.
Mama scolded Jason for days about his interactions
with the ox. While she tended to his bruises, she
cautioned him that though he felt like he could sedate
the beast for a moment, he would never be able to
change its true nature. Much like elastic stretched to
capacity, the beast would always return to what it was
made to be.

Wesley's thoughts soon subsided and he turned to
look at his brother. He saw Jason sitting back against
the bed with his eyes closed, probably thinking
about *her*.

Wesley's silence finally broke. "Be careful with
Detra," he said, "I don't trust her."

In the middle of Miracle Village sat a colossal sized
church. It was a simple one-room edifice lined with
benches. On its roof stood a large white cross that
was the focal point of the town. The building served
many purposes including holding town meetings,
serving as a refuge space from natural disasters, and
of course hosting church services. The doors of the
church were always open, even in the middle of the
night and Jason found himself there tonight. Mama
always insisted that they attended church. The three
of them went to church for prayer service that
evening because to Mama, prayer service was not an
option, it was an obligation. Although she could not
monitor their church attendance abroad, while they
were here with her, she would make sure that they

went. Mama knew her prayers were what kept the boys safe, especially when they were miles away from her. She would cover them with her morning and evening prayers, and her words would always return to her fulfilled.

As the service ended, Mama and Wesley left Jason to spend some time alone while they headed home. All the other prayer service attendees also made their way out, and now Jason sat alone in the empty space, eyes closed, facing the altar, talking to God. Trying to at least. He hoped God would answer his prayers or at the very least, simply hear him. Jason felt a familiar breeze sweep by him and suddenly felt her presence.

"Detra," her name fell from his lips.

"I didn't mean to interrupt your prayer," she said apologetically.

"I'm not even sure if I'm really praying. Maybe I'm just thinking."

"All the same," said Detra assuredly.

Jason's eyes followed Detra as she approached him and sat next to him on the bench.

"Detra," he hesitated a bit before continuing, contemplating whether to ask his question. He then mustered up the courage and continued, "How do you know that God hears you?"

"The same way you know that I can hear you right now," Detra replied.

Jason chuckled a bit. She answered the question as he expected her to, quickly, without hesitation, and with an unshakeable assurance.

An unexpected silence fell between them, and it remained for a few moments. The church was dark and empty. Every cricket chirping, stray dog barking, goat bleating, or banter from a neighboring home faintly echoed into the church. Jason stood up and paced over to the window to look. The church sat at the highest point in the village, and from this view, he could see the many colorful homes in the distance. It was getting late and most of the lights were off, but some homes were using the last bit of solar energy to power them through the last few moments of daylight.

He spotted his own little red house in the distance at once. He wondered what Mama and Wesley were up to now as he stared out into the night. Knowing Mama, she was probably getting food and clothes ready for the next day, while Wesley continued with his studies. Jason knew he should be doing the same. The MCAT's were soon approaching and he figured that he should probably be getting a head start on studying as well. Wesley, the responsible studious one, was most likely going to pass the LSAT's on his first try, and Jason was already proud of him. But instead of studying with Wesley, Jason would much rather be here, in this space, for now. It felt good here, with her.

He turned around to face the church and he saw Detra's eyes fixated on him. The moon light reflected through the window made her eyes look like dark shining orbs and he could see that there was a question burning within her. However, she could not bring herself to say the words. He figured he could answer her unspoken thoughts.

"My father, from what I can remember, was a very strict man," he spoke, "a cold man. Had he lived, I doubt he and I would've gotten along very much. He probably would've had a better relationship with Wesley than with me. Wesley was and still is more obedient of our father's wishes. Me, not so much. One thing I will always credit my father for, is that he was a man who provided for his family. Anything my Mama needed for herself or for us was taken care of even before she could say the word," he paused to see if Detra was following. She was.

"We were living in New York," he continued, "that's where he worked. He was saving up to build a home out here in Haiti; my father made it a point to build his home out here. The principle of returning to your roots, establishing yourself there, and advancing your own people was something he would preach relentlessly. When he finally felt like he had saved enough money, he moved the entire family to Haiti. He built this huge, stunning home, over the top even. A home that I'm sure most people wouldn't even believe exists in Haiti.

I remember being in awe of our new house, I almost didn't believe it was truly our home. But my brother and I didn't stay long. Father agreed to let us stay with our aunt in America to finish our schooling, so long as we always return home, which we always did, every summer. But then…"

"Your father died from cancer, and it happened quickly," Detra finished his sentence for him in a factual tone and it troubled Jason a bit.

He looked up at her to see her eyes still on him, glistening as she listened.

"Yeah, that's right," he answered her. Jason figured Mama told her this. "And shortly after that, the house he built was destroyed in the earthquake. In a matter of a few short years, my Mama lost everything."

Jason crossed his arms over his chest and looked up at the church ceiling as he fought back tears.

"My dream, Detra, is for my Mama to see us make it. Both Wesley and I. I want to make her proud. I want her to see us become the men our father wanted us to be. Great providers. It is my hope to restore everything that she lost, everything that my father worked so hard for."

Detra finally pulled her eyes away from him and asked, "Why are you telling me this Jason?"

Jason closed his eyes before answering Detra. He took a deep breath and could smell the onset of rain in the atmosphere. He opened his eyes and surely enough saw a brief flash of lightning in the distance.

"Just in case God doesn't hear my prayer," he finally spoke, "maybe you can tell Him for me."

The soft pitter-patter of rain hitting the roof of the church quickly filled the stilled space.

Chapter Five

Wesley approached his mother from behind and hugged her. The sudden contact made her jump and she dropped the dish she was washing into the washbowl, splashing the water all over her apron.

"Oh baby, you scared me, look what you made me do," she turned around to show Wesley the mess on her apron. He in turn just chuckled in amusement.

"Oh you're laughing at me?" she threatened as she flicked her wet hands in his direction. Wesley shied away from her, trying to shield himself from the water.

Mama laughed at her silly son, but then opened her arms wide for a hug. Wesley came in and rested his head on her shoulder. He almost bent over in half, as Mama was a whole foot shorter than he was.

"I love you Mama," he told her as he hugged her tightly.

"Uh oh, what happened?" she pulled back from him to get a good look at his features. His forehead was pleated with creases and his eyes were burdened with worry.

"I'm concerned about you," he admitted.

"Oh, my honey," she kissed his cheek, "there's nothing to worry about baby."

"Mommy, be honest with me, are you sick?" he took a hold of her hands, not minding the wet suds that now spread onto his own. He did not stop thinking about the possibility of his mother's illness since yesterday after Jason told him Detra was a healer.

"Now why would you ask me that baby? Because I wasn't feeling well the other day? I was just having a bad day baby, no need to fret," she said reassuringly.

"Why don't you just come live with us in New York?"

Wesley figured that she would be better off being with them in The States. This way they would be able to take care of her should anything happen. Besides, Mama would undoubtedly have access to better medical care should she become ill.

"The United States is just not for me baby, Haiti is my home. Your father and I agreed a long time ago that Haiti is and will always be home."

Mama had always been skeptical about moving to The U.S. She knew that her children wanted her close but living there was just not an option for her. She felt America had the tendency of luring their visitors in, fooling them with glitz and glam, enticing them with a certain lifestyle, only to spit them out tired, overworked, and jaded. She had witnessed it happen to many of her old friends that left Haiti only to return home wanting to stay for good. Her late husband firmly stood on the principle of cultivating your home, and for that reason ultimately built his home in Haiti despite working abroad. After the earthquake, her sister-in-law had opened up her home in New York to her, Jason, and Wesley. The boys were already staying with their aunt for school, but Mama refused to move. She wanted to live in Haiti. She would visit them from time to time, but only visit. She never saw herself staying permanently. Haiti was home.

Wesley knew that further pushing the issue of her moving would prove to be futile. He decided it was best to get to the heart of the matter, the core of his worries.

"Mama, is Detra here to help make you feel better when you get sick?" he asked.

"Baby, Detra is here," Mama hesitated for a bit before continuing, "she's here to watch over me."

"Mama, why do you need watching over if you're fine?" Jason questioned. "I just don't understand, and I don't feel comfortable with her being around here."

Mama's tone softened. "I get it baby; you want to protect your mother. But it's *my* job to protect *you*, I'm *your* mother."

"All I want is for you to be safe and healthy."

"I am," Mama said. "I am."

Wesley shook his head, as his shoulders slumped, "I can't understand why Jason likes this woman so much."

The two moved over to the couch and took a seat. The plastic covering the mustard yellow piece of furniture squeaked as they took their positions next to one another. Wesley laid his head in his mother's lap as she stroked his hair away from his face. Her baby; they grew up so fast, she thought. Mama remembered the days she would whip both of them for stealing keneps from the market.

Now here they were, bigger than she was. Wesley had always been the more sensitive of the two and could always be found right under her. Anything Mama needed, he was there, and she loved it. Mama's heart always melted for Wesley. However, the time had come for him to stop living his life for her. He had to let go, they both did. The time would come one day when they would have to let go of her for good.

"He's intrigued," she finally replied. "You know your brother; he loves the unknown, he's very curious."

"Yeah I know." Wesley said. "But I told him, he should be careful with her."

A thought crossed Mama's mind that made her uneasy, "Wesley?"

"Yes, Mama," he noticed that she stopped stroking his hair.

"Is that where Jason is now? With her?" she questioned.

Wesley shrugged, "I guess. He said they were going to the lake."

Mama's eyebrows wrinkled. She noticed that Jason spent quite a lot time with Detra, but the lake was a little far from the house for her liking. It was beginning to get dark and Mama could not help but wonder what Detra was up to with her son.

Detra laid flat on her stomach across the grass as Jason sat beside her. They had been sitting by the lake for a while now. The pair watched time elapse as the sun set and the day made way for the night. The lake that once glistened with the orange rays of the setting sun was now gleaming with the blue tint of the moonlight. Jason sat leaning back on his elbows just staring at the moonlight illuminate the ripples the small fish made across the glistening lake. The two actually had not spoken much in the hours they spent together. Both just sat quiet continuing to be lost in their thoughts. For Jason, just being around Detra was enough for him. Peace and tranquility always seemed to accompany her presence. To him, she felt warm and that was quite a contrast from his normal day-to-day life. Sometimes it all became too much to bear; schoolwork, heavy course loads, studying, and the stress of it all. Detra provided him with much needed rest. He felt as though he could stay here with her forever.

Jason turned his head when he heard a sigh leave Detra's lips. She was rubbing her face and her arms across the grass. It was something she had been doing periodically since they were out there, and Jason could not take his eyes off her.

Per her request, they spent most of the day going about town, eating more fruits, discovering different tastes, and debating her favorites.

By late afternoon, Jason decided to take her to one of his favorite places, Lake Azuei. The lake was a place he used to frequent during the summers as a child. He had found a little patch that had not been deforested and it became his place of peace; somewhere he could clear his mind. It had been the first place he ran to after learning of his father's death. He recalled that day so clearly. Everyone was home waiting for the moment to come as they all knew it would. His father was weak and tired as he had been that whole summer, but something was different about that day.

Every other day, his father had a fight in his eyes, but that morning, it seemed as though that light had dimmed overnight, and by midday, he was gone. Not knowing how to deal with the grief and shock, Jason ran towards the lake where he discovered the forested part that led right into the opening of the water. Jason remembered not being able to make sense of his emotions that day. A furious mixture of pain, fear, confusion, disbelief, and guilt were wrapped in a blanket of sorrow. It was Wesley that found him; a tear streaked, muddied up, and disheveled mess. The two rested there in stillness until it got dark. Before actual nightfall, they returned home with the weight of the world on their shoulders. Ever since then, Jason made it a habit to visit the lake every summer. It had become his place of solace. Being there with Detra gave him more peace than ever before. This was pure bliss.

"What are you doing?" he asked her, smirking. He knew she was only exploring more of what he had taught her.

Detra proudly answered, "Feeling the grass against my skin."

He grinned as she confirmed his suspicions.

"Feels good?" he asked.

"So good," she smiled that heart-stopping smile he loved. "There's so many good things about this world."

He watched her lick her lips. They were stained with the residue of the mangoes they had just shared. Her first mango, which she had immediately declared as her favorite fruit yet. Jason enjoyed watching her sloppily devour the fruit, leaving traces of orange around her lips and juice streaks dripping down her arms. She was a mess, a beautiful mess. After consuming the first one, she immediately asked for another. Of course, he obliged without hesitation, only this time, she refused to share with him. Greedily, Detra ate the mango all by herself, even tossing the dry seeds behind her like a professional when she was finished.

Jason got up and headed towards the lake and Detra quickly sat up to see what he was doing. She watched him, as he washed his hands in the water before returning to her. He approached her and wiped his wet hands across her mouth to remove the mango residue from her face. He then grabbed her hand and wiped them clean of the sticky mango juice.

Detra wanted to shy away from his touch, but just could not bring herself to do so. His touch felt good. He was so bold and fearless with her and she treasured it. When he was done, he laid back against the grass, hands folded behind his head, staring up at the night sky.

"Thank you," she uttered, before joining him in stargazing.

They laid there together for a moment, saying nothing. Jason noted that there were mosquitoes everywhere but curiously enough, they stayed away from him and Detra. Not one of them approached them or dared bite them. It was very peculiar. The mosquitoes in Haiti were known for being ruthless, relentless, and savage. Jason could only credit their strange behavior to Detra's presence.

"Why don't you speak the language of your people?" Detra's voice penetrated through the stillness, startling Jason.

He took a minute to think before responding, "I know a few words here and there, but I never truly learned it. Both of my parents spoke English since they lived in America before moving back to the island. Wesley and I grew up abroad, so we never really had to learn it. We only needed to know just enough to make it through the summers in Haiti."

"You should learn it." Her recommendation was absolute.

"Why'd you say that?" Jason inquired.

"Your language is your identity Jason. You are recognized by your tongue. It is your history and your progeny. It's a part of you that if not practiced, is lost forever," she said in that all-knowing tone.

Her words filled his ears with familiarity. His father always insisted that the boys spoke *Kreyol*, but it never interested him nor Wesley. Their father would lecture them on how Haiti was one of the few nations that still had a language they could call their own. "How will your children know where they come from?" Jason could hear the bass of his father's voice echoing in his mind.

Before letting his thoughts get the better of him, Jason decided to turn the question on Detra. "So what language do you speak?" he asked her.

Detra's reply was lacking. "I speak many languages."

He rolled his eyes at her curt answer. "Ok, so what language do they speak in heaven?" he specified.

Detra paused before replying, "The heavens speak one language that is understood by everyone."

Jason was perplexed, "What does that even mean?" he asked.

"Look at the sky Jason, the stars," he followed her instructions and gazed up at the stars. They shone the brightest out here, more than anywhere else he had ever been. "Everyone in the world sees the same sky and stars that you do, but they hear and understand them according to their own capacity."

Jason paused and let himself get lost in the night sky.

"Close your eyes Jason."

He did as she instructed.

"Do you hear that?"

Jason was unclear about what he was listening for.

"Do you hear the worship Jason?" Detra asked.

Jason was confused. There was no way Detra could hear the church all the way out here.

"Do you hear the crickets chirping, the fish swimming in the water, the birds singing, the insects crawling, the leaves rustling?" she rephrased her question this time.

Still unclear where she was going with this, Jason answered, "Yes, I hear them."

"Well, that's a language called worship," she clarified.

"And what are they worshipping?" he inquired.

"The Master of course." Detra spoke as though he should have already known. "Believe it or not Jason," she continued, "everything in nature is continuously worshipping The Master."

Jason could not say that he fully understood everything Detra was saying. He did, however, enjoy listening to her impart her knowledge, even if they were too grand for him to grasp. Almost losing his train of thought, he quickly remembered his next request.

"Tell me about heaven," he said.

Detra questioned him, "Why do you ask me about heaven Jason?"

For once, Jason felt a knowing reply fall from his lips, "Because I know that's where you come from."

"What makes you say that?"

He turned and smiled at her, "You're an angel Detra."

Detra chuckled a little, "And how did you figure that out?"

"Something so beautiful could only come from heaven. You have healing capabilities and you talk to God. What's more telling is that He talks back."

He paused a little and smiled, "You don't know anything about grass or fruits," he almost laughed. "You're not from here. You must be an angel."

Detra sighed, "I can't say that I'm not."

"It's ok; I know you would never tell me directly," said Jason.

She smiled, "And I also can't tell you much about heaven either."

Jason's eyebrows furrowed, "Why not?"

"The secrets of heaven are reserved for those who dwell there," Detra's voice now low.

"And do you *dwell* there?" he asked, skeptical of her responses.

"I can't…just like I can't dwell here."

"Then why are you here?" he probed.

Detra wanted to divulge everything to Jason but instead simply said, "I'm on assignment."

"For my mother?"

Detra hesitated a little before confirming with a slow nod. Jason wanted to ask the multitude of questions that encircled his mind but was afraid of the answers. Therefore, he opted to stop there.

"I need you to take care of my mother," he finally spoke his thoughts.

"I will."

"She's everything to me, I can't lose her," he continued.

Detra stared at his profile and wanted nothing more than to touch him. It was an instinct that she never felt before. These feelings were not only new but alluring as well. She almost reached out to touch him but then he turned his head her way and she quickly retracted her hand.

"Jason, you do know that everyone has their time when they must go?"

"I wish that time never comes for my Mama," Jason's voice was dripping with sadness.

"You can't disrupt the order of things Jason. One day she's gonna have to go home."

She watched as his whole demeanor instantly changed, "That's easy for you to say, you're probably never gonna die," he said to her.

Detra took a second to look at Jason before she spoke up. Unsure of whether she should be revealing this, she blurted out, "One day The Master won't have any more use of me."

Jason understood that that was the closest thing to dying an angel like Detra would ever experience. "I don't wanna talk about this," he stated, "I hate thinking about this stuff."

She could not help it this time, she had to touch him; she had to soothe him. She reached for his hand and grabbed it. It was the first time that she initiated contact, and he felt the difference. She slowly rubbed her fingers against the back of his hand. The feeling of peace he always felt when near her intensified with her touch and he yearned for more, he needed it. He grabbed her hand tighter and pulled her close to him. She landed with her chest against his and the sigh that left his lips told Detra that he felt her energy. Only she could provide that sweet peace for him. Jason felt a healing that transcended the physical and reached the mental and spiritual. She wanted to stay there and pour more of herself into him, but knew it was impossible. She quickly pulled back from him and watched him come down from the momentary high she provided him. He opened his eyes and the expression on his face confirmed he did not understand what just happened to him, he was lost for words.

He let out a huff before abruptly standing up and throwing off his shirt.

Jason made his way into the lake for a quick dip still trying to shake his current confusion. He looked to the water to soothe the constant wheels turning in his mind.

Even though he knew that the legends in Haiti warned against going into the lake, especially at night, being there with Detra made him fearless.

Detra watched his bare back as he moved towards the placid body of water. She knew he was trying to make sense of what had just happened. Detra could not let Jason continue touching her because his touch, though subtle, ignited her flesh in ways that were unfamiliar. She knew what was happening to him, but she was not sure what was happening to her. She watched as Jason walked into the lake and dipped his head beneath the water before coming back up. His hair was now damp and hanging over his head. Detra just sat back and admired how beautifully his skin shone now wet with water. In the few days that she knew him, Detra felt drawn to Jason.

It all started with the way he first looked at her when she opened up Mama's door. His stare never faltered and that instantly drew her in. She tried to stay away from him, she knew better than to get close, but this time was tough for her. His spirit was reaching for her, and her instincts told her to reach back. It was an unspoken calling and Detra wanted nothing more than to answer it. Her carnal instincts were leading her into uncharted territories. She wanted to indulge in these new sensual feelings. She longed to taste him much like the kenep and sugar cane. It would be another first for her, but she was sure she wanted it to be with him.

Before she could control her desires, she stood up, peeled her dress off, leaving her body bare and nude. She slowly walked into the lake and reached out to Jason. His eyes absorbed all that she was. He never even noticed how quickly all the fish, tadpoles, and every other living creature within the lake scurried away from her. His eyes were fixated on her beauty from head to toe. Every inch of her was perfect. Her skin was flawless, and her soft curves were nothing short of enticing. Jason's eyes locked onto Detra's as he drunk all of her in. He could not seem to focus on any one thing; his eyes darted from her breasts to the apex of her thighs and he enjoyed seeing all of her covered in that lovely brown skin. His stare finally rested on her sweet face. He reached back out to her and took hold of her hand. Immediately, he felt that same peace transcend through him again.

"I didn't mean to upset you," she spoke.

He had almost forgotten what they were previously discussing. When the memory returned he replied, "I'd die for my mother."

"I know," Detra said sweetly.

He pulled her in close, and their chests met once more. This time skin to skin. They both let out a heavy sigh at the touch of one another.

The warmth that emanated from both their bodies was shared. Where the heat began and where it ended, neither could tell because it was indistinguishable. Her embrace felt so right to Jason and in that moment, nothing else mattered. Everything else faded around them and it was only the now that made sense. Strange and beautiful as it was, it solidified everything for Jason. For Detra, all of this was novel to her. The coolness of the water against her skin brought a sensation that she never felt before. At the same time, she felt strangely familiar. That feeling coupled with Jason's skin on hers was sending her to new heights. She had never felt someone like Jason. Never on a spiritual level and definitely not on a physical either. She undoubtedly wanted more.

"Jason," she whispered, "I want to taste you."

Jason pulled back to see her eyes. He saw the light of the moon reflected in them along with a deep desire for him.

"Make me taste you like you made me taste the mango," she repeated.

Jason happily obliged. He could never say no to her. He pushed the stray hairs away from her face, cupped it in his large hands, and leaned down as his lips touched hers. Slowly he puckered, which drove her to do the same. She pulled back smiling.

"More?" he asked.

A simple nod confirmed that she wanted more. Their lips met again, but this time, Jason used his tongue to part her lips. He gently nibbled on her bottom lip and taught her to do the same. He tasted better than kenep she thought. Jason lit her up and she felt like she was on fire for him. They continued to kiss slowly and sensually. She wanted to bask in the moment because she knew soon enough they would have to stop. She greedily sucked on his soft lips until he started to take control. For Jason, he could not believe that he was kissing his angel. Everything about this felt right. His blood ran hotter and his skin tingled from their contact. He was high and wanted to stay that way forever.

Detra suddenly pulled back from the kiss. The imminent interruption she knew would come had arrived. There was a disturbance in the water, and as they both looked down they saw a snake circling them. It writhed and coiled in the water, slithering its venomous tongue towards them. Jason began to panic, but she held him close.

"Don't be scared Jason, he won't hurt you," she told him.

Even though she tried to reassure him, the fear in his eyes was ever-present. She turned to the snake and hissed at it and to Jason's surprise, the snake quickly slithered away from them. He was stunned to see the snake back down so obediently.

Who is this woman? His thoughts cut short when Detra's lips were back on his. Slowly, they massaged and melded back together, re-introducing their tongues as they indulged in each other's essence. A sudden violent wind started blowing water and leaves around them in the lake. It placed them at the center of a small whirlpool accompanied by a tornado of leaves. Detra groaned and pulled away from Jason.

"We have to go," she told him and grabbed his hand leading him onto the grass. After getting dressed, they headed home, once again leaving Jason with more questions than answers.

The two made it back to the village just in time. Miracle Village had a strict curfew and if they had not made it back before the guard closed the gate, they would have a lot of explaining to do. The pair entered Mama's house hand in hand, laughing. They both came to an abrupt stop when they saw Mama standing by the door awaiting their arrival. She took in their wet, dirty, disheveled appearances and shook her head in dismay. Her stern eyes almost froze Jason in place, but he could not let that steer him away from her. He let go of Detra's hands and went over to kiss his mother on the cheek.

"Hey Mama," he said sweetly.

"Hey my baby. Are you okay?" Mama's words flowed to Jason, but her eyes were fixated on Detra.

"Yes Mama, of course," he replied.

"Alright honey. Do me a favor;" she asked, "give me a moment to speak with Detra."

Jason looked back at Detra and smiled, "Yes of course."

Jason kissed his mother again before saying goodnight. To Mama's surprise, he went back to Detra and kissed her on the cheek as well before exiting the room. Mama turned back to look at Detra. She stared at her intently for a moment before speaking up.

Mama's tone was low but direct. "Stay away from my son," she warned her.

Detra smirked, "You dare speak to me in that manner?"

Chapter Six

Mama stood her ground facing Detra. She just witnessed Jason's affectionate display; holding Detra's hand, kissing her on the cheek, even laughing with her. Mama could not believe her eyes and she did not like it one bit.

"What are you doing with Jason?" she questioned.

Detra's frame was statuesque, awaiting Mama's next move. "You dare question me?" she said.

The tension in the room was thick, due to the powers at hand pushing and pulling against each other. There was minimal movement between the two, but the surge of energy in the atmosphere made it evident that the two were at war.

Mama knew that compared to Detra she was powerless, but she would give her all in the fight for her son. Detra, on the other hand knew that there was no reason to fight, she had already won.

Mama's better judgment told her to back off, but her love for her son overrode all her fears. "Why are you always around him?"

"He came to me. Your son, he wants me," Detra said knowingly.

"He doesn't know who you are."

"But you do, so I suggest you stay calm," Detra retorted.

Mama quickly shot back, "No. Stay away from my baby."

Mama tapped into the power she held as a woman, the power she had as a mother, that natural instinct she had to protect her child and prayed it was enough.

"Are you giving me orders?" Detra asked. "I only take orders from Him. He is my only Master. You and your kind have no say in what I do. I want Jason for me, and I will have him."

"No you won't!" Mama's voice was now elevated.

"Remember that you've been shown favor. An exception was made for you. Don't ruin it," Detra quickly reminded Mama.

"If I knew this would be the cost, I would've never asked for this," Mama's resolve sunk a little as she thought of Detra taking her son. Tears escaped her eyes and silently drifted down her cheek.

Detra, however, showed no remorse. She turned around and made a move towards Jason's room. Her mission was to spend the night with him. Mama however had to give it one more try. She lunged towards Detra and grabbed hold of her arm.

"I said leave him alone!" Mama shouted.

Mama knew she was taking a big risk. Touching Detra in that way could mean the very end of her life but she was willing to take the risk. Detra turned back to look at Mama, now annoyed that she would not stop protesting. There was no fight. There was no competition, no bartering. She wanted Jason and she would have him. If Mama did not back down, then she better be prepared to face the repercussions of her erratic actions. Detra frowned but gently removed Mama's hold from her arm before speaking up.

"Again, you speak to me as if you don't know who I am." Detra continued, "Have you once again mistaken me for one of your kind? You know what I am capable of doing. I am before your time and so will be after. You ought to show respect before your favor runs out."

Detra once again turned around to go back to Jason.

"You're right," said Mama, again interrupting Detra, "I know exactly who you are, I know exactly what you do. You are a killer! And because of that, I won't let you near my child."

Detra had had enough! She whipped around swiftly and a wind swept through the house, blowing in the drapes and knocking down Mama's favorite vase. Mama shielded her eyes as her hair blew wildly around her face. The wind settled, and she noticed that a picture frame had been knocked down. Mama picked it up and eerily enough, it was an old picture of Mama holding her sons when they were still babies. The frame had cracked, and it split right through Jason's face. This picture was one of the few things she was able to salvage from the debris caused by the earthquake. She was grateful, it was the last remaining baby picture she had of the boys. The only one that survived the disaster. She used to keep the photo in her old Bible, but recently placed it in the frame the boys got her for Christmas. Mama clutched the now broken frame to her chest and looked up to see Detra approaching her with menacing eyes.

"I'm no killer. Your kind are killers," Detra hissed.

As she neared Mama, Detra's shadow loomed behind her and it grew larger and larger with each step. The shadow had completely coated the floors and walls of the room.

Her shadow stopped reflecting her figure. Instead of outlining Detra's petite physical frame, it now reflected her inner being. The shadowy presence outsized the space and bore wings ten times the size of an eagle's. The dark wings flexed as Detra continued.

"Your people are so wicked that you invent new ways to kill and make up new reasons to do so. Some of you even end up killing yourselves!" Detra was now face to face with Mama, "No, I'm no killer. I just guide people from one life to the next. I am a messenger. A powerful one at that. You will do to remember it."

Mama could feel the fear welling inside her but could not back down; she clutched the broken picture frame to her chest. She fought back tears before weakly uttering her final plea, "Just, leave him alone, please," she begged.

Detra looked back at Mama and she felt sympathy for her. It was such an unfamiliar sensation. Emotions altogether were new to Detra. She was accustomed to receiving orders and carrying them out, without emotional involvement. This time was different and the more time she spent in this body, the more human she felt.

It began with that first taste of kenep. Tasting the fruit ignited a slew of human sensations, both physical and emotional. She saw how sweet it tasted and immediately wanted more.

She could not fight it, the food here was delicious, and she craved it. With every new indulgence of her appetite, she became more human, and with humanity came emotions. Emotions for one of their kind, Jason; now *he* was sweet. The feeling of his skin on hers was incomparable to anything she had ever felt. His lips on hers felt better than heaven and much like the fruit, she wanted more of him too. Detra wanted to indulge in him until her belly was full. He was hers to have.

"I love him," said Detra.

Her words almost knocked Mama off her feet. Before she could help it, a smile was tingling the corners of Mama's lips, and laughter spilled from her mouth. Her previous fear had quickly turned to amusement. Mama could not believe what she was hearing. This had to be a joke. Though the current situation was far from a laughing matter, she just could not control herself. She tried to remain calm, but here she was neck thrown back, cackling at Detra's statement.

Detra's demeanor now hardened. "You dare laugh in the face of Death?" she questioned Mama.

Mama never meant to be so audacious, but she was completely beside herself.

"Love?" Mama scoffed, "What do you know about love? You take love from people. You destroy lives!"

"You and I both know that's not true," Detra said. "I make love real. By me, love is proven."

"How could you know what love is when you're so selfish and greedy? You're never full, never satisfied, always searching for more, and attempting to satisfy a never-ending hunger and unquenchable thirst. But let me tell you something Detra," Mama said mockingly, "you won't take my son."

"Yes I will," snapped Detra.

"Not before his time, you won't!" Mama's tone was more than daring, it had become almost warning.

"You are in no position to argue with me," reminded Detra.

Mama nodded her head in agreement. Detra was right. How could she win against Death? Although it meant risking her life, Mama continued, "Taking Jason for yourself would be the most selfish thing you could ever do. Love would never do that. True love requires sacrifice and I'm sure you know nothing about that."

Mama was taking a big risk speaking to Detra in this manner. Truthfully, Mama was not scared for her own life; her time would soon come. She instead feared for Jason. She wanted to protect him and she vowed that she would do so in both life and death.

Mama glared at Detra, "Do whatever you want to me, but don't take my son, don't take my baby. I'd die a thousand deaths before I let you do that."

It was about six days prior when Mama flew out of bed and started her day as she normally would, cooking and cleaning. Today was not a normal day by any means. It was special for several reasons. Her sons were coming to visit and Mama could barely contain her excitement. They were trying to surprise her with an early summer visit, but Wesley could always be counted on to spill the beans ahead of time. He could never keep anything from her and she loved it. Jason would undoubtedly be mad, but it did not matter. Her sons would bicker and fight, then make up as always. Though a surprise would have been nice, she would have missed the opportunity to cook their favorites. Rice, chicken, macaroni pie, couscous, fish, and salad aligned the kitchen table. Mama even picked up their favorite juice, *ju grenadia*, or passion fruit juice for them to enjoy with their meal.

Mama lived alone for a while now. After her husband died, and her sons went to school abroad, she had been mostly on her own. It was almost a year since she laid eyes on her boys, and the anticipation was almost too much to bear. Mama checked their old room to make sure it was still intact. It looked as if they had not been away for a day. She was certain their long legs would barely fit on their twin beds by now. She took a moment to fix the checkered patterned sheets on their beds and then straightened out the picture frame that covered the hole in the wall. She chuckled to herself thinking back to how the hole got there.

Jason thought he was slick covering it up with the picture frame. She never told them that she knew all about how their play fighting caused the damage to the wall. Actually, their play fighting had caused quite a bit of damage to the house over the years. Mama ultimately decided that it was okay to let this incident slide.

Mama closed the bedroom door and checked on the food one last time. Jason and Wesley were due here in a couple of hours. She washed her hands and did some last minute tidying before retiring to her room.

Mama reclined in her bed to take a quick nap before they arrived. She was feeling a little weak and she thought that maybe some rest would ease the aches she felt. She tossed and turned uneasily trying to grasp the moments of sleep that kept slipping from her. Once she was finally able to ease into a light rest, she was gently awakened by a soft voice.

"Denise Pierre. It's time," said the voice.

The voice was sweet and soothing, and it had a calming effect on her. She should have been afraid at the sound of this strange voice, but there was a peace in the atmosphere that would not allow her to panic. Mama flicked her eyes open only to be blinded by a bright light. A luminescent flash of lightning lingered in the room. She placed her forearm against her eyes to shield them, but she kept them open in order to catch a glimpse of the figure before her.

"Who are you?" she asked.

The light dimmed and a figure stepped toward her. She could make out a face. Dark eyes and thick dark lashes framed a very beautiful face. Hair like wool cascading down to her shoulders with skin the color of honey. The most prominent feature were her wings. They were huge, and dark, with feathers that glistened in the sunlight. Once spread, they took over the entire room. Mama was in awe but still could not tell what was going on. The figure neared her bed and sat on the edge.

"I am the angel of Death," she grabbed Mama's hand. "You are dying."

Chapter Seven

"Wait, wait, I'm dying?" asked Mama to the angel sitting on the edge of her bed.

"Yes, you are," the angel replied, grabbing hold of Mama's hand.

Mama sat up facing the angel. "How can this be? I'm not sick and I'm not that old."

"It's your time. Death never needs a reason to take you. You have accomplished your mission here on Earth. Your purpose has been fulfilled."

"But wait…," Mama said trying to interrupt the angel once more.

The messenger said to Mama, "It's time to move on to the next life, to go home to heaven. I will take you there. Do not be afraid."

Mama was in shock but oddly enough at peace. She could not believe how easy this transition was. She never imagined it would be like this. There were times she even feared dying but this was simple and easy. A part of her did want to go, to move on and see what the next life had in store for her. The part that was tired and thirsted for rest, the part of her that could no longer fight the sleep. Mama wanted to succumb to the weight of her eyelids and let the darkness take over, but something held her back.

"Wait, please," said Mama. "Of course I want to go to heaven. But my boys…my boys are on their way here. They'll be here any minute now and, I at least want to see them one last time. Will you grant me that before I go? Please?"

Mama would not fight it. She decided that if this were her time, she would just let it be, but she had to see her sons one last time. She needed to hug them and kiss them just once more in order to go in peace.

The angel breathed in deeply. By the look of skepticism etched across her breath taking features, Mama already knew the answer would be no.

"I would just hate for them to find my body here," Mama continued, "they wouldn't be able to handle it. Please," she begged.

"That is not my decision to make. It's His." The angel pointed upwards as she spoke.

She breathed in and out again while Mama watched in awe. She never thought Death had a face and if it did, she never thought it would be a woman. Mama imagined Death as a grotesque monster yet here she was as the loveliest of angels. She awaited the angel's words once more.

With closed eyes, the angel said, "He has said, 'my good and faithful servant, I will grant you this one last request. However, my angel is to stay with you. She shall guard you.'"

As the angel finished speaking, Mama heard a heavy knocking at the door. Jason and Wesley had arrived.

Since their conversation in the church, Jason sensed a shift in Detra. Last night at the lake solidified that there had indeed been a drastic transformation in her. She woke him up early the next day asking him to take her to the Earthquake Memorial. It was so early in the morning that Jason was sure the rooster had not even crowed yet. However, he could hear the birds chirping in the distance. Detra's face was a mere few inches away from his and he had a feeling that she had been there for a while watching him sleep. He turned his head to see Wesley still in his bed snoring away, something he wished he were doing right now.

But one look at Detra's lovely face immediately changed his mind, he realized that he would much rather be awake with her instead of asleep. His eyes adjusted to the light and he was able to see clearer now. The early morning sunrays crept through the window and the sheer pink curtain filtered the natural light. It gave Detra's rich skin a beautiful rosy glow. Her eyes were filled with a wonderment and curiosity that Jason just could not deny. Before his mind could process what was occurring, he had already agreed to Detra's request and in a few minutes was up, dressed, and on his way out with Detra close by his side.

Jason was able to hire a man to help them take the journey to the memorial location. Rony was one of the few people in the town who had a vehicle. Providing rides for others in the village was Rony's way of making a living. He was all too happy to drive Jason and Detra around for a small fee.

The Earthquake Memorial was a few hours' drive from the village by car and Detra and Jason spent most of the ride in silence. As they rode out to town, Jason was surprised at how many people were up and active that early in the morning. Merchants were already out setting up their stands while children in their plaid uniforms were on their way to school. Vehicles adorned with paintings of Bible verses, athletes, celebrities, and even political figures made their way around the city bright and early. The morning hustle combined with the scantily paved city streets made for a lot of damage.

Both the foot and vehicle traffic, created a mini dust storm that irritated Jason's and Detra's eyes. Rony noticed Detra and Jason struggling to see and thoughtfully offered them sunglasses. Jason could not help but chuckle at the way Detra looked sporting a fresh pair of sunglasses. He figured he looked just as silly in these old school 90's retro lenses.

They soon pulled up in front of The Memorial only to find the gates locked. Jason began to groan in annoyance, but before the sound left his lips, a young boy ran down the hill ready to meet them with the keys to the gates. Apparently, the neighboring village were officiated the guardians of the memorial. Jason and Detra were granted access and entered the space. What began as a few wooden crosses planted in the earth to honor the dead was now an entire monument. An unfinished project, but still breathtaking. Erect columns stood in a circular structure while a large boulder posed in the center of the circle. Near the center were two poles proudly bearing the blue and red Haitian flag. The flags endured some wear and tear over the years and although they were slightly tarnished, they still waved in the wind with pride. Within the circular formation were plaques engraved with words of encouragement decorated with mournful black bows. In the centerpiece's distance stood a black marble archway adorned with metal angels serving as guardians of honor. The marble arch was the entrance leading guests towards the mountains, which Haiti is most known for. Haiti, *Ayiti*, means land of mountains in Taino, the language of the indigenous people.

At any point on the island, you are sure to be surrounded by mountains. They stand majestically as protectors of the land and their beauty is unmatched. However, none stood in comparison to the ones at the memorial site. These mountains had peaks that seemed to kiss the sky. They were a direct connection from Earth to heaven, and it was particularly fitting given the circumstances. These mountains were the final resting place of the majority of the earthquake victims. Many native Haitians were buried in the heart of their land and in a beautiful, bittersweet twist; their death brought rich, fertile life into Haiti's most glorious signature.

Detra stood at the center of the structure in silence. She was taking in the splendor, breathing in its essence and accepting the miraculous cycle of life and death. For once she realized her role in this sequence. Although she always knew her importance, a new knowledge had set in. She began to grasp an awareness of her effect on individuals, families, and nations. So she stood there, learning. Detra remained standing there for what felt like hours. Jason was convinced that she was talking to God again. He noticed the winds picking up as time passed and he thought it best to stand back and not interrupt.

Being at the memorial site was a bittersweet experience for Jason. It was his first time there as well and it was the first time that he truly mourned the lives lost.

At the time of the earthquake, he was living in New York, worried sick about his mother's safety. When he finally received a phone call letting him know she was alive, he was so elated that he never took time to mourn for his people. However, coming face to face with the victims and standing on their burial ground, Jason became overwhelmed with emotion. He felt a soft warm hand wiping away tears he had not known were there. Detra tiptoed and kissed him on his cheek before letting him hold her close to his chest. She wanted to comfort him with the knowledge that everyone who died in the earthquake was doing well in the next life. She wanted him to know that the worst part was over, but she knew it would be of no use. What was just a simple concept to her was a literal matter of life and death to him. She knew that her words would mean nothing to him until he realized them for himself one day. One day soon she hoped. Detra stood still and silent and held him there until he was ready. Even as the wind picked up, she stood resilient, determined not to move until Jason was ready. The Master was calling her, but she wanted to remain with Jason. It was not until the strong gust caused the flags to violently flap against the flag poles that they decided to leave. They hopped back into the vehicle with their patient driver and began the long journey home.

Chapter Eight

Wesley wiped the sweat from his brow as he dusted off his hands on his worn jeans. Wesley's pants were marred by mud, dirt, and grind, worn and torn in several places and absolutely not presentable to the public eye. Yet they were his favorite article of clothing, they were his gardening pants. Mama woke him up early that morning and had him accompany her to the community garden.

Mama had a green thumb, maybe an entirely green hand. For this reason, the people of Miracle Village unofficially elected her to be the proprietor of the community garden. The garden was a highlight in the town and their very own project. It was one of the few aspects of the village they felt truly belonged to them.

It was not simply given to them, they worked for it, they cultivated it, and they were proud. Though many people in the village worked in the garden, Mama was here the most. It became another home to her, after the church of course.

Gardening was a habit Mama picked up after her husband died. Her neighbor, seeing her grief, invited Mama to come help her in the garden where she grew her greens. Somehow, as Mama dug into the tough ground and as she used her hands to open up the hard earth, she was able to release the tension that knotted her joints. The hard work helped her release all the sadness and worries that choked her. It was a healing process. Each time she planted a seed and buried it in the earth, Mama felt a new sense of purpose. Few things gave her more joy than seeing the first green bud of life days after the seed's initial burial. It unexpectedly gave her hope. She found herself returning to her neighbor's garden more often than she probably ought to, but the sweet elderly woman enjoyed the company. The more Mama tended to her neighbor's garden, the more therapeutic it became. It was then that Mama realized her hidden talent for the craft. Before she knew it, Jason and Wesley were joining her early in the morning, planting. It quickly became their family time and it was sacred for all three of them. After a few weeks, the boys were also thrilled to see their hard work beautifully blossom into its own little paradise. They were taught things in the garden that they would never learn at school. These were the lessons that often contained no words, rhyme, or reason.

Even though Mama was no longer as agile as she used to be, she continued gardening. For her, the greatest lesson learned in gardening was that planting a seed and cultivating the earth, was life's twisted way of helping her deal with the death of her husband. In gardening, from death came life. The death and burial of one seed turned over and birthed the life of many more. It was the universe's metaphor, and it meant even more to her now that she was facing her own death.

"Mama, where's Jason?" asked Wesley, breaking her thoughts.

"I saw him leave early this morning with Detra, I'm not sure where they went," she said.

The silence between them was a testament as to how uncomfortable they both were with Jason's newfound friendship with Detra. Wesley felt that Jason should be here with them instead of out with that strange woman. It troubled him, and he could tell that Mama too was perturbed by his absence.

"Mama," Wesley paused, "do you believe in reincarnation?"

Wesley's question was not as random as it seemed. He had been ruminating on the concept for quite some time, and he wanted Mama's opinion on the matter, even though he already had an idea of what she would say.

"Reincarnation? What is that darling?" she questioned.

Wesley explained to Mama, "That's when someone dies, but they come back to life in the world as a different thing. A dolphin, a dog, or mosquito maybe."

Mama laughed and she wondered what in the world were they teaching her children up at that American school, "No baby, I don't believe in reincarnation. I believe that once you die, that's it. You've lived your life and it's on to the next world."

Wesley was in no position to argue, so he just took his Mama's word as so.

"Mama, in my heart, I want to believe that you will never leave us, but if you ever do, I hope you reincarnate and come back to us."

Mama laughed, "What do you want me to come back to you as baby?"

"A hibiscus flower," said Wesley.

His answer was direct, straight forward, and without hesitation. It was clear that he had already given it some thought.

The hibiscus. That was Mama's favorite flower. Beautiful bright red, with a few gorgeous stems of yellow pollen emanating through its center.

The petals were as soft as clouds, and the scent, more divine than any perfume she ever smelled. If plucked correctly, the hibiscus offered a sweet juice right at its stem. Mama often felt that the hibiscus was God's gift especially made for her.

Mama wondered why all of a sudden Wesley was asking her about death and reincarnation. She figured that he probably felt it coming for her, and her heart broke for her baby. She knew it was soon to come and she wanted to take their pain away before they ever felt it.

Mama had to be upfront with Wesley, "Baby, flowers die too."

"Then I would just plant you again and again and watch you grow each time," he said.

Hearing that warmed Mama's heart. The love she had for her sons was unmatched, but their love for her was deeper than she ever thought. Their love was a flame that enveloped her heart. The thought of leaving them behind tore her apart. However, she rested in the knowledge that the three of them would never lose their love for each other, not even in death.

"Darling, I'm already planted, right in here," she said poking the left side of his chest. Mama playfully wiped some dirt on the tip of his nose as he shied away.

"So tell me, since you believe in this reincarnation thing," she said, "what did your father come back as?"

"Father is a tree," a proud Wesley stated.

That somehow made sense to Mama. She understood how Wesley could see his father being big, strong, and rooted like a tree. Her husband being reincarnated as a tree would mean that he would still be a provider; a provider of shelter, shade, oxygen and even fruit. She kind of liked the idea and decided to continue with her probing.

"What will you and your brother come back as?"

"Jason is going to be a dog."

"A dog?" Mama asked. The shock was clear in her voice.

Wesley quickly followed up his initial statement. "Not like the dogs here. The dogs here remind me of squirrels. I mean an American dog. The kind that are a part of their families. They're everyone's best friend, they're trusting, and adventurous."

Mama's chuckle was soft, "I can see that."

"And me," Wesley continued, "I'll be coming back as a…," he thought for a while but could not come up with anything.

"You're a bull!" A voice resonated behind them.

The two looked up to see Jason standing there with his hands in the pockets of his own pair of dirty gardening jeans. The three of them laughed together, internally deciding that Jason was probably right about Wesley.

After sobering up from her laugh, Mama finally said, "Jason, you came back to me darling," reaching out her muddy hand to him.

"Always," he replied as he took her hand and kneeled next to her in the soil.

Upon returning to Miracle Village from the Earthquake Memorial, Jason changed his clothes and hurried to the community garden. He knew there he would find Mama and Wesley. Detra asked him to stay with her, but this was an appointment that he could not miss. This was family time and it was sacred.

Jason quickly kissed Detra's sweet lips to ease the sting of rejection and rushed over to be with Mama and Wesley.

The three of them continued their gardening, their laughing, and their teasing right into the afternoon of the day.

Chapter Nine

It was unbearably hot today on the island. The hard work Jason put into gardening with his family that morning only made things worse. Jason was in search of a way to cool down. He ended up finding temporary refuge sitting under one of the large trees in a nearby field. The shade from the tree combined with a glass of his mother's ice-cold all-natural passion fruit juice, or *ju grenadia*, did the trick. He looked up and saw Detra standing on the porch staring at him. He smirked to himself, as he knew she had become just as intrigued by him as he was by her.

Her stare was shameless, and she never bothered to look away when their eyes connected. As for Detra, she just wanted to be near him. This humanity thing forced her to discover the importance of proximity.

Usually, she would be able to feel people, sense them, and know their presence. Jason, however, taught her that physical proximity and a simple touch proved to be crucial.

Detra looked a little bit further past where Jason was sitting and could see the village playground. There were a few old men engaged in a game of dominoes; their animated banter over the game amused her. Not too far from the elders, a few children were running around on the playground. Some of them played on the swings soaring high above the clouds while a few others took turns on the seesaw. Detra could hear their laughter from where she stood and thought in her experience, children loved life the most and yet were the least afraid of her when she came to them.

Before she became lost in another thought, Detra realized that she was walking towards Jason. The body she inhabited tended to act out of its own volition and Detra's control was lost. No longer shielded by the shelter of the house, she could freely feel the sun beating on her bare back. Her backless, halter top dress provided the perfect canvas for the sun to shine its beauty. The sunrays made her skin tingle, and she took a moment to bask in the warm sensation. Detra continued walking across the grass barefoot until she was face to face with Jason. She wasted no time sitting on his lap, straddling him.

She was more comfortable with him now and wanted to get even more familiar. He wrapped his arms around her waist and pulled her close to him. She reciprocated wrapping her arms around his neck.

"How was the rest of your morning?" he spoke. His words were muffled as his face was buried in her neck.

"It went well. I stayed here after we returned from The Memorial and I spent a lot of time thinking about you," replied Detra.

"What about me?" he posed.

"I was thinking about the way you make me feel."

"And how do I make you feel?"

Jason finally removed his face from Detra's neck and came up for air. He was now facing her and was dangerously close to her lips just as they had been the previous night.

"No, just that. You make me feel. And it's wonderful," replied Detra.

Emotions, feelings, and love, they were such wonderful things to experience. As a timeless being, she never understood how humans were so drawn together, so connected. Now she knew what it felt like and she had Jason to thank for that.

"You make me feel too," he said.

Detra noticed beads of sweat forming on Jason's forehead. She wiped her hand across his head only for it to return to her moist.

Detra looked puzzled, "Why are you wet?"

Jason chuckled, "I'm sweating, because I'm hot."

By now, the sun had reached its highest point in the sky and its proud rays were relentless. Even now, Jason was still sweating from working in the garden.

"You're sweating too," he said as he traced one lone finger down her collarbone and into her blouse.

His finger came back wet with the moisture of her sweat. She had not even realized she was sweating. Now that Jason brought it to her attention, Detra could actually feel the moisture seeping through her pores, forming on her skin, and pooling into beads. One of those beads rolled down her back and soon she felt Jason's fingers catching it before it reached the hem of her dress. The gesture made her hotter than the heat wave. He grabbed his cup of juice and tilted it to her lips, urging her to take a sip so she could cool off. Though the melted ice cubes watered down the flavor, she could still delight in the sweet taste of the passion fruit.

Jason brought the cup down from her mouth and before he knew it, Detra had unabashedly pressed her lips to his. They both moaned at the contact. She could taste the blend of passion fruit mixed with the flavor of his lips and she savored it. This felt better than the sun beating on her back. It felt like the sun was bursting right through her insides and its heat radiated in her womb.

As she pulled back from their exchange, she whispered,

"I want to be with you always."

In awe that an angel may consider leaving heaven for him, he asked, "You'd stay here with me?"

"I can't," Detra sighed, "but I want you to come with me."

Jason, perplexed, questioned her further. "Come where?"

"Just come be with me," said Detra.

Jason was unclear as to what being with her would entail, however he knew it required him to leave this Earth, and he was not prepared for that.

"Detra, I want to," Jason began, "but I can't. I can't leave my mother or my brother. I have to stay here with them."

"Do you love them?" Detra quickly asked.

The question threw Jason off guard a little. "Of course I do," he replied.

"I love you," was all Detra could manage to say.

Before he could even respond to her declaration of love, Detra began kissing down Jason's neck to his heart. She placed her lips on his chest, right on the surface that encased his heart. As her mouth lingered there, she could feel the thud of his heart beat against her lips. It was a melodic drumbeat that penetrated her eardrums and resonated to the temporary heartbeat she possessed. The rhythm of her heart and his were almost synchronized until his heartbeat began to accelerate. She closed her eyes to relish this human experience. Never before had she paid much mind to the heart. When she took people from this life to the next, she never stopped to gauge the corporal reactions of the deceased. That was not her concern as she dealt primarily with spirit. The body was left behind to return to the dust from which it was formed. When she took on this assignment, she was lent this body to encase her spirit form. It happened instantaneously, as soon as The Master agreed to give Mama more time. Detra barely realized that she was no longer just spirit; she was now spirit and body. At first, she was unimpressed feeling that the physical world had limited her. She was unable to move as freely as she did in spirit. It took her some time to get used to all that came along with this body, but after a while, she slowly began to adapt. Detra never thought of the form as more than just a shell. However, Jason showed her it was far more than just that. He made her see how wonderful the human body truly was. How amazing it was that from dust, all of these sensations could arise.

The burn of the sun's rays, the wetness of water, and the taste of different flavors were all foreign to her prior to this experience. Even her desire to be with Jason was something Detra never imagined she would experience. What is more peculiar is all these desires vanished once the spirit is called home. Humans had but a moment to enjoy this, and Detra was grateful that she was given that chance with Jason.

Detra was thankful for Jason. He was wonderful, and she wanted him as hers forever. She too wanted to show him some things about her world but knew that he was not ready. He may never be ready, no one ever really is. How would she ever get him to agree to leave everything behind and willingly come with her? How could she tell him that she was not just an angel as he suspected, but was in fact the Angel of Death? Though he had introduced her to Life, Death was her assignment. It was in fact more than just her assignment, it was her purpose, it was her entire being, her identity.

Detra continued pressing her lips to his heart. As he leaned his head against the tree, closing his eyes, Jason allowed the odd sensations to take over his body. A heat emanated from his heart and flowed through his bloodstream. The warming sensation became embedded in his bones and yet was accompanied by a coolness on his skin. Curiously enough, he also felt a numbness overtaking his body.

He felt himself painlessly and slowly slipping from this life. Detra felt his heartbeat dangerously slow down under her lips. She knew that if she stayed there, his heart would eventually stop and he would be hers. She lingered just a little more but then suddenly broke the connection. She had to will herself away from him. She did not want him this way. It was not who or what she was. Messenger, not killer, she silently reminded herself. The power was there, but not the authority. The authority belonged to The Master and she needed to obtain His permission in order to move forward.

Slowly, Jason's heartbeat retuned to its normal pace and Detra closed her eyes once again appreciating the rhythm.

"What are you doing to me?" he uttered as he blinked his eyes open. He was undoubtedly groggy from the almost out of body experience he just had.

"I won't hurt you, I promise," Detra said.

She kissed his throat and then laid her head to his chest to listen to her favorite sound, his heart. After a moment, she asked the question she meant to ask him since last night at the lake.

"How do people make love?"

Jason chuckled. He lifted her chin and pressed a gentle kiss on her lips.

"Like that?" she asked.

"That's how it starts," he stated. "You want me to show you?"

Detra mulled over his words as she looked into his eyes. She did want to try, with him. Knowing she had but so much time left in this body, she wanted this experience before returning to her spirit form. Detra wanted to know what it would feel like with Jason. Actually, she thought that his offer was brazen, given his knowledge of her being otherworldly. Although she was stunned that he would even consider it, the fact remained that she was the one who brought up the subject. She wanted it without a doubt, but she knew she would be unable to carry out the fantasy.

"I can't," Detra finally said after a while, "I'm not allowed to defile the body that was lent to me."

Jason could see the disappointment in her eyes. Admittedly, he too was disappointed as well.

"Well I can show you the next best thing," said Jason with a tone of excitement in his voice.

Detra skeptically responded, "And what is that?"

Jason began shifting her off of him so he could rise, "I'll show you how to dance."

"Dance?" Detra questioned, "I don't believe I'd be good at it," she said hesitantly.

147

"That's why I'm gonna teach you," said Jason as he grabbed her hand to pull her up. He held her close by her waist and whispered, "You don't need to be nervous, just trust your body."

With that he tugged on her hand to lead her back towards the house, almost running in eagerness. Once they arrived on the veranda, Jason pulled out a handkerchief to gently wipe the sweat off her brow and his. He then pulled out his phone and pressed play on a sweet old tune. The sound of a melodic guitar rift accompanied by a heavy base quickly filled the space. The song was a traditional Haitian kompa song that his father used to listen to in their home when he was younger. Though he never fully learned the lyrics to the song, Jason was proud to say that he had learned to play the instrumental on his guitar.

Detra stared in amusement as Jason comically swiveled his hips while playing an imaginary air guitar. As the soft crooning of a man in love took over the song, he extended a hand to her and pulled her close.

"First you start with a little two step, side to side," Jason explained as he demonstrated.

Detra awkwardly followed his instruction.

"Remember to trust your body," reiterated Jason.

This was a new concept for Detra, as this was a new body. She wondered what would happen if she completely let go and let herself just be in this moment. She had already experienced great pleasures in this body, and she was curious to see what joys dancing would bring her.

She closed her eyes and let Jason take the lead as he in turn let the music lead him. They continued with the two step until Jason steered Detra into a spin. The move surprised her and she could not help but laugh.

"Are you enjoying this?" asked Jason, knowingly.

Her bright smile answered his question. The two continued to dance on the porch and Jason was just as amused as Detra. He was not quite sure, but he could have sworn that he saw small wisps of light about her as she twirled to the music. They were already on their third song when they clumsily became entangled. Detra ended up with her back to him as he wrapped his arms around her waist. He hugged her tight against him and kissed her bare shoulder.

As they gently swayed to the soft tune, it appeared that the leaves on the nearby tree were also swaying along with them. The leaves just as quickly began to rustle, and they soon began to shake almost violently. Detra closed her eyes, took a breath, and broke loose from Jason's embrace. It was clear to Jason that something in her demeanor had abruptly changed. She had become almost as rigid as she was when they first met.

"Are you the reason why it's been so windy lately?" he asked her.

"Yes," Detra looked down as she replied.

"Why?"

"That's The Master telling me to remember who I am."

Jason let out a breath, "We're not supposed to be doing this, are we?"

"No, we're not, but I'm the one at fault. You won't have to pay for this."

Jason knew that it might be impossible for him to actually be with Detra physically. How could an angel and a human ever be together? He knew nothing about the spirit world or the heavenly realms and was unsure what the repercussions of being so close to an angel included. He did not know whether "The Master," as Detra called Him, approved. His disapproval made it unclear as to what his fate would be. All Jason knew was the here and now, and that included Detra. He decided to enjoy this moment with her. He would deal with what is to come when the time came.

"How long are you staying here?" he asked her.

"Until my assignment is over."

Jason wanted to ask her what exactly her assignment was. However, knowing it was about his mother made it too much for him to bear. He knew that knowing more information would do him more harm than good, so he decided to leave it alone and remain in the now.

He approached her, grabbed hold of her hands again and said, "Spend the night with me."

Detra looked up at him and considered his offer. Beyond him, she could see in her line of vision, Mama inside the house staring at her with a disapproving glower. Mama had been watching them for quite some time now. Though she was in awe to see her son unknowingly interact with Death so pleasantly, Mama knew that ultimately Detra could not be trusted.

"No my love," Detra finally responded, "spend the night with your mother, and your brother. You and I will have our time."

Chapter Ten

"Jason, bring me another board," Wesley yelled back as he used all his might to keep the windows closed. Using all of his strength to push the window panel back, Wesley awaited Jason's return. The wind was beating heavily on their little home and their best bet in keeping the house from falling apart was boarding up the windows and the doors.

Jason brought over a board to the window and helped Wesley nail it shut. With the last of the windows boarded up and the door securely shut, Wesley, Jason, and Mama would be able to weather the storm. They had become used to the intensity of tropical storms on the island, however this storm was anything but normal. There was no rain, lightning, or thunder; just wind, it was barely a storm at all.

Haiti was not particularly known to encounter wind storms, and this was a violent one. Palm trees threatened to snap at any moment at the hand of the wind. Every animal in the village, the dogs, goats, birds, and insects sought shelter from the storm. Everyone in the village was shook with fear at the first signs of the dry storm. It had begun early in the evening and now it was at full force with no signs of stopping. The elders in the town whispered that there was a force among them. The wise ones knew its source but dare not speak against it.

Once everything was sealed up, the three gathered on the couch with Mama sandwiched between the brothers in silence. Mama could do nothing but hold her sons close to her. Tears welled in her eyes as she knew her time was up.

Wesley broke the silence as he glared at Jason, "It's all your fault!".

"What?" Jason answered, taken aback.

Wesley's voice was now raised, "You heard what I said Jason. You know who's doing this."

"Hey, stop it Wesley." Mama tried to put an end to the argument before it escalated any further.

"You don't know what you're talking about Wesley," Jason replied.

"I don't?" questioned Wesley. "All Detra has done since we got here is cause trouble. Mama's illness, this absurd weather, the old woman and her dead brother, shall I go on? I told you to stay away from her, but you never listen."

Jason's voice now matched his brother's. "Shut up Wesley!"

"No fighting tonight babies," said Mama. Her patience was noticeably wearing thin.

"We came here to see Mama, and instead of spending time with your brother and your mother like we planned, you've been stuck up Detra's ass!" Wesley continued despite Mama's warnings.

"ENOUGH!" she yelled.

"But Mama, it's true," said Wesley.

"Wesley please baby, let it go."

If this was going to be her last night with her babies, Mama didn't want any fighting. She wanted to cherish her last moments with her boys. She wanted to make sure that they knew she loved them. Before the words could even leave her mouth, Jason beat her to it.

"Mama, you know I love you," he said, "I would never leave you. You know that right?"

"Oh my baby," she said stroking his handsome face, "of course I know you love your Mama. And I love you too. Both of you. So much. I live for you. You boys mean the world to me. And please know, I will never leave you either, no matter what happens," she squeezed them both to her chest.

"But Jason baby, you have to know that Wesley just cares about you," she continued. "He wants you to be safe. He's trying to protect you."

"I don't need him to protect me."

Wesley scowled.

"Stop it right now! You both need each other. I wish I could stay here with you and protect the both of you forever. But I can't. I'm not gonna be here with you forever. Sooner or later I won't be able to be here for you. Maybe sooner," she bit back a tear, "so I need you both to take care of each other, protect each other, love one another. There's a reason why you two are so connected. You guys have to stay together. Promise me that you'll stay together."

"I hate when you talk like that," said Jason coming in for another hug.

"Me too," Wesley agreed.

"Just promise me," she reiterated. She just needed to hear them say it. It was the most important thing to her in this moment.

"We promise," they both agreed.

Wesley nestled into her bosom, "I'd die for you Mama."

"Shhh, don't say that baby," she grabbed his face between her palms, "I need you to live. I lived my life so you could live yours."

She kissed his cheek and then grabbed Jason to do the same.

The two decided to let the issue go and just coddle into their mother, their queen, their life source.

That night as the storm raged on, the three of them all squeezed into Mama's old bed. Mama remembered how when they were younger they used to do this when they were scared of the lightning and thunder caused by the tropical storms. They would both act tough like they weren't afraid, but as soon as that thunder roared and that lightning flashed, the two would bury themselves under the covers and hang on tight to Mama's arms. But this was no tropical storm. And now they were much bigger so the fit on the little queen-sized mattress was much more snug. But Mama didn't mind. She wanted to spend the night with her babies.

As they drifted into a sleep, Jason couldn't help but think that Wesley was right. He knew for a fact that the wind was caused by Detra.

More so, Detra speaking to God. He wondered what they were arguing about. This had to be an argument; these winds were too strong to only depict a normal conversation. He figured that Detra had come to the end of her assignment. The thought alone made him scoot closer to his mother and hug her tighter before falling asleep in her arms.

Mama awoke to a voice calling out to her. That same voice from that night. The storm was still weathering outside the sealed doors and windows. Mama could hear the wind howling and the branches snapping all accompanied by a deep whistling moving through the air. Yet all that noise was dwarfed by the faint whisper that called her name. She climbed out of bed, leaving her boys peacefully asleep. Following the whisper into the living room, she came face to face with Detra. Mama took in a gasp of air as she stared at Detra who no longer inhabited the body Mama had become familiar with. In its stead, Detra was encased in light with wings that spread throughout the room. Her eyes were bright, her skin glowing, and her hair flowing in the breeze that her essence provided. She was ethereal, and Mama was once again in awe. Detra had become Death's full-blown creature. She was majestic and beautiful but Death nonetheless. Mama knew that her time had come, and she was ready to go willingly. She approached Death, but the words that escaped Death's lips stopped Mama in her tracks.

"I have an offer to make you."

Mama hesitated a little, "What kind of offer?"

"How would you like to live a little longer?"

Mama was skeptical about Death's offer. She knew there had to be a catch, but she was willing to hear her out anyway.

"Of course I would love to be here a while longer with my children," Mama said.

"I've received orders from The Master to only take one from this household."

Mama shook her head knowingly. This was the catch she was certain would come. "It would have to be me," she confirmed.

"It doesn't have to be you."

"You're not taking anyone else from here; you're leaving with me and me alone." Mama knew Death wanted to take Jason instead, but Mama would never let that happen.

"You may want to think about it. Do you remember the time I healed you? Your body was failing you and I saved you from me."

"And what are you saying?" Mama feigned interest. She did not care about anything else Death had to offer.

"I can assure that you shall never fall sick for the rest of your days. You will be in optimal health and your body will never fail you. When the time comes for you to transition again, I will make sure that it is peaceful."

"No," Mama's reply lacked hesitation.

The frustration Death displayed did little to stir Mama. She stood her ground and refused to let Death take her son. Death flapped her wings creating a gust of wind about the little house.

Detra's true form spent the majority of the afternoon pleading with The Master. As Jason surmised, their debate caused the windy chaos amidst the small town. She begged The Master for permission to take Jason for herself, but He would not allow it, as it was not Jason's time yet. Death then proposed living here on Earth with Jason but that too was out of the question. The Master needed her for His purposes.

After Death's proclamation of love, The Master finally agreed to a compromise. As not to disrupt the order of the universe, He permitted one life for another. Death could not take both Mama and Jason; she was permitted to take only one and she was satisfied with the exchange.

However, as it was Mama's life in question, The Master ordered her approval first. As much as Jason belonged to Him, Jason also belonged to his mother. Death could not take Jason before his time; not without Mama's permission.

If Death learned anything about humans, it was that they loved life and would do anything to preserve it. She never understood the concept but after experiencing life for herself, she could see why humans held on so tightly to theirs. She figured it would be a simple exchange offering Mama more life in lieu of her son. However, her biggest fear had befallen her. Mama was not in favor of the deal. There was no way that Death could defy The Master and go against Mama's wishes.

"The Master gave me permission to take Jason," Death said.

Mama's face was ridden with skepticism as she questioned what she just heard. "What?"

Death bit her tongue before continuing, "But only with your approval."

Mama chuckled. "Did you really think I would give it to you?"

Death attempted to reason with Mama. "In return, you get what everyone in this world wants; more time to live."

"I would love more time to live, but I would want it to be with my children. If you take Jason, then I would spend the rest of my days wishing I were dead anyway. What kind of life is that for a mother?"

"I love him," pleaded Death.

"No, *I* love him. That is why I am willing to give my life for his. I would sacrifice myself for both of my sons without question."

Before Mama knew what was happening, she heard a terrible exclamation emanate from Death's chest.

"I want him!" she cried.

The notion of Death fearing anything was absurd, but here she was standing in fear before a mere human. How had it come to this? The concept of love had rendered her weak and it stripped her of her power and pride.

"If you love my son, let him live." Mama approached Death and fearlessly grabbed her hand. "Do you love my son?" Mama asked.

Nodding surely, Death replied, "Yes I do."

"Then you must let him go. You have to give him the chance to enjoy the life he deserves. A life filled with joy and growing pains. Don't take him away from his mother and his brother. Allow him his destiny. Give him the gift of life. That's what love is."

Love. Death was mistaken all this time on what it really meant to love others. Jason showed her the blissful side of love. The kisses, the hugs, the passion, the heat and warmth of being together.

The feeling of skin against skin, the sweet taste of pleasure, the sweetest fruit there ever was. The love that made two beings inseparable. The inexplicable ecstasy of a deep connection. The discoveries that came along with learning one another as they built a future. It was all so wonderful, and she wanted to have it forever.

Mama now showed her the other side of love. True love meant putting others needs and wellbeing ahead of your own. It encompasses, pain, longing, and sacrifice. Mama's wise teachings coupled with Jason's love and affection completed Death's lesson on love.

Death let out another cry as her wings flexed down in grief.

"What you're feeling," said Mama, "is what we feel whenever you take someone we love. That's called pain."

Pain. With that, Death flapped her wings and flew out of Mama's small red home. She flew over the town of Miracle Village and neighboring communities. Her wings finally brought her to rest at the center of a large, circular, unfinished stone structure; the Earthquake Memorial. Death immediately fell to the ground as anguish gripped her. Enveloped in her frame, she grieved the loss of her beloved Jason. Pain over their separation caused her to cry out in mourning.

A recollection flashed in her mind. Death saw herself slowly making her way towards a dying man on a bed in his home. The time had come for her to collect his soul. As she passed by his family members, for the first time, she recalled passing by a young boy. Even then, she remembered Jason looking at her; almost as if he saw her even though she knew, he could not. At the time, she had no idea who this young man was or the impact he would have on her. Passing through that home was just an order to carry out, now she realized its significance.

After a moment, Death pulled it together and stood up. These human emotions were taxing, and they weighed on her. It distorted her sense of self and compromised her being. She hovered over the memorial and faced the mountains that enclosed the bodies of those who perished in the disaster. She remembered being called to collect all who had lost their lives that day. It never occurred to her what they went through or how those affected by these deaths were dealing with their sorrow, even now. She knew everything would be okay but that did little to comfort the people on the island. Their pain did not stem from the earthquake's destruction but more so the pain of continuing life without the people they loved most. For the first time in eternity, Death mourned for their lives, and all the lives she ever collected. She came to the realization as to why life meant so much. It was less about self, and more so meant for others.

Death returned to the house in Miracle Village only to find Mama already waiting on her. In silence, and complete defeat, Death accompanied Mama to her room to say one final goodbye to her sons. As they slept, Mama bent to kiss both of their foreheads, whispering words of love in their ears.

Death spoke up, "I too would like to say goodbye."

Mama moved over and allowed Death to approach the boys. She sat near Jason and hugged his unknowing body as she cloaked him in her wings before pressing a kiss to his cheek. Death stared into Jason's beautiful face while she stroked his hair. What is the point of loving passionately, sharing affection, and making sacrifices, only to lose it all in the end? She questioned if it was even worth it. The former Detra looked into the face of her love and she decided that the answer was yes. She would never trade this experience with Jason for anything.

"My love," she whispered to Jason as she stroked his face. He stirred but he did not wake, "Thank you for showing me what love is. In return, you have been granted long, prosperous, and abundant life. I will protect you all of your days and not a single hair on your head shall fall without The Master's permission. Any evil that attempts to rise against you, will fail.

I also vow to protect your future wife and children and your children's children, and so forth until the end of your line." Death pressed her lips to his. Rising, she whispered, "Taste me my love," as her lips brushed against his.

In that moment, she inhaled Jason's essence into her being. His chest deflated as his spirit left him. She closed her eyes, letting it internally marinate before breathing back into his mouth. His chest expanded as he received the gift of life, peace, and protection.

Death pressed one last kiss to his forehead before moving on to Wesley.

"I now understand you only wanted to protect your brother," she said to him. "You love him. The same promise made to him, you too shall receive. The power you two hold together shall increase as your days increase. I promise I will never come in between the two of you again."

She kissed Wesley's cheek and turned to Mama, "Ready?"

"Yes," said Mama as she released the breath of air she had just taken in.

Death grabbed Mama's hand and the pair began their ascension to heaven.

Wesley stirred awake the next morning. His stretch felt a little too comfortable. The night before, he fell asleep in a cramped bed but now he had a bit more room in the bed to move.

He pealed his eyes open to see that indeed the bed was missing a body. Jason was still asleep beside him, but Mama was no longer laying there.

"Jason, where's Mama?" Wesley asked as he shook Jason out of his slumber.

"I don't know man," replied Jason as he wiped the sleep out his eyes. "You know she's an early riser."

"I don't know man, something feels different." Wesley was unable to shake the feeling that something was up.

The brothers got up and started searching the house for their mother. As Wesley roamed around the home, he noticed that the picture frame they gifted Mama for Christmas last year was out of place and broken. He made a mental note to get her a new one. He picked it up to put it in its proper place and a shiver ran down his spine. Now more nervous than before he cried out "Mama!" as he continued his search. Worry began to set in when he did not find her in any of the rooms in the house.

After searching inside the house for some time, Jason stepped outside and was instantly blinded by the shining sun. The storm the night before made it feel as though the sun would never shine again. Yet here were blue skies and the brightest of lights. The sun's rays were enough to make him feel as if the storm had never even happened.

He looked into the distance and noticed a gentle breeze flow through the clothes hanging out to dry on the clothesline. Behind one of the white sheets pinned to the line, Jason made out a figure. Approaching the sheet with caution, he whipped the sheet to the side only to see that smile that he loved most. Her smile made all the pain go away and brought him comfort as long as he could remember.

"Mama! What are you doing hiding out here?" he exclaimed.

"Oh my baby!" she opened her arms for a hug, "I was just messing with you. Just playing a little hide and seek with my boys."

"Wesley, I found her!" Jason called back towards the house. Wesley soon followed his brother's voice and stepped outside to join in their embrace.

"Mama, you scared me. We couldn't find you this morning," said Wesley.

"Honey…you know I would never leave you," she said kissing his cheek.

"I know Mama," Wesley quickly replied.

"So what do my babies want for breakfast?"

The two started rattling off a full menu for her as they made their way back towards the house. Mama laughed at their gluttony before making them promise that both of them would help cook and then clean in the aftermath of their feast. Wesley rushed inside to get started on the meal, leaving Mama and Jason strolling behind. Before stepping inside, Jason turned to Mama and asked a question that had been on his mind since the previous night.

"Mama, where's Detra?" He noticed her absence from the house and he even felt a shift in the atmosphere.

"Um, well, baby," Mama began, "she had to go."

"Her assignment is over?" asked Jason.

"Yes, yes it is," she answered with a look of satisfaction on her face.

"What was it?"

Mama sighed a bit and cocked her head to the side, "She was sent here to learn about love."

Jason was taken aback, he was not expecting that response.

"So that's it, I'm never gonna see her again?" he asked, disappointed that he might have missed the chance to be with his angel.

Mama looked at her son, the man that unknowingly captured Death's heart. She knew her baby boy was special, but she never imagined this. Her son was the man that Death fell in love with.

"You'll see her again baby just not any time soon. Your paths will cross again one day, a *very* long time from now."

Ironically enough, Mama figured in Jason's line of profession, he might be in contact with her more often than most. However, that did not worry Mama at all. She knew he was protected. Mama looked into her son's eyes; she could not help but be thankful to God for yet another chance at life. He rewarded her for her bravery in the face of Death, and the sacrifice she was willing to make for her sons. Most importantly, The Master repaid her example of true love with life. Long, prosperous, abundant life.

The End

Nadjeda Estriplet

Keep in Touch

miraclevillagebook@gmail.com

www.miraclevillagebook.com

www.instagram.com/miraclevillage

www.facebook.com/MiracleVillageBook

13491780R10104

Made in the USA
Middletown, DE
17 November 2018